Whose Town?

LORENZ GRAHAM

Whose Town?

Foreword by Rudine Sims Bishop
Afterword by Ruth Graham Siegrist

Boyds Mills Press

Published by Boyds Mills Press, Inc.
A Highlights Company
815 Church Street
Honesdale, Pennsylvania 18431
Printed in China

Publisher Cataloging-in-Publication Data (U.S.)

Graham, Lorenz B.
Whose's Town? / Lorenz Graham ; foreword by Rudine Sims Bishop. — 1st ed.
[208] p. : cm.
Originally published: NY: Thomas Y. Crowell Company, 1969.
Summary: David Williams must decide which course of action to take in the African American struggle for Civil Rights.
ISBN 1-59078-163-5
1. African Americans — Fiction. 2. Race relations – Fiction. I. Bishop, Rudine Sims. II. Title.
[F] 21 2003
2002117208

First Boyds Mills Press edition, 2003
The text of this book is set in 12-point Palatino.

Visit our Web site at www.boydsmillspress.com

10 9 8 7 6 5 4 3 2 1 hc

*To the brave young people of America
who are seeking answers to hard questions.*

Foreword

Lorenz Graham believed with all his heart that "people are people." That statement seems obvious on the face of it, but behind it is a lifetime conviction fed by both happy and unhappy experiences with people in many places in the world, and by a strong religious faith. When Graham was twenty-two years old, he dropped out of college in California to become a missionary in Monrovia, Liberia, in Africa. Before he left the United States, he had read and been told many things about what Africans would be like. People used words like "savages" and "heathens" and "uncivilized," and warned him of danger. At first he carried a weapon when he went out at night, but he soon discovered that he was "safer on a dark trail in Africa at midnight than [he] would have been on a well-lighted street in an American city." He learned that Africans were very much like the people he had known in the United States—ordinary people living ordinary lives. It was that experience in Africa and in France, where he spent some time recuperating from malaria, that made him decide to become a writer,

> with the one message that "People are People—white, black and all shades and colors between, African, American, French, German. The cultures of the world, and the conflicts when we who call ourselves people refuse to recognize that those whom we call enemies are also people, very much like ourselves, with desires, needs and hopes which are quite identical to our own desires and needs and hopes.

When he later wrote a book about an African boy and his adventures in daily living, he was very pleased when a newspaper reviewer wrote that an American reader would recognize the African boy as "just another fellow." That was exactly what Graham had hoped for. In the context of the United States of his day, Graham's idea that "people are people" had an added meaning. Not only did he want his readers to understand that people the world over are basically alike, he wanted them to understand that all people are deserving of basic human rights and social justice. He wanted to say through his novels that all people have a right to equal treatment under the law and the right to "life, liberty, and the pursuit of happiness" as stated in the United States Declaration of Independence.

Lorenz Graham's four "Town" novels—*South Town*, *North Town*, *Whose Town?*, and *Return to South Town*—not only relate the story of David Williams and his odyssey from a small rural southern town to the North and back again, but also chronicle the turbulence and social change that took place from the mid-1950s through the end of the 1960s. These novels are set at a time when social conditions were grim for many African Americans, especially in the South. In spite of those conditions, however, people like the Williams family and their neighbors tried to live ordinary lives in places like South Town. They went to church and worked hard and tried to see that their children would grow up to enjoy better lives. Although they sometimes were forced to give in to some of the discriminatory customs of the day in order to survive, they always held onto their sense of dignity and refused to lose hope. Sometimes, conditions became unbearable, and some families packed up and moved to the North, where life was in some ways better, but where different problems awaited them. This was the era of the mid-century Civil Rights Movement; and reading these novels about an ordinary, but in some ways extraordinary, African American family reminds us not only why that movement was necessary but also how difficult the struggle has been.

It is hard to imagine what life must have been like in the rural South in the mid-1950s, but perhaps a look even farther back in time will help. History tells us that for more than two hundred years, between 1619 and 1865, most Black people in the South had been enslaved. One excuse some people had made up to justify slavery was that Africans or Black people were inferior to white people—not as smart, not as capable, in fact not quite as high up on the ladder of humanity. Therefore, these white supremacists believed, Black people did not deserve the same rights as whites. Even after the Civil War and the emancipation of Black people, even though the Constitution was amended to make Black Americans citizens with the right to vote, even a hundred years later and beyond, many white supremacists held on to those antiquated and false ideas.

So, especially in small rural towns in the South, "Jim Crow" laws, or segregation laws, were still affecting daily life in the 1950s. Back in 1896, the Supreme Court had ruled that it was legal to separate people by race, provided the separate facilities were "equal." Even though "black" and "white" facilities were never really equal, Black and white people were forced to live separate daily lives: separate water fountains, separate waiting rooms at bus or train stations, separate schools. And invariably the "black" or "colored"—as they were called then—facilities were inferior. *South Town* is set just after the Supreme Court of the United States had declared that "separate but equal" schools were inherently unequal, and had ordered the states to desegregate their schools "with all deliberate speed." But it would take years for that ruling to take hold and make a practical difference.

Furthermore, even when segregationist practices were not written into law, they were "understood." In *South Town*, for instance, it was understood that white boys and Black boys would not swim in the same place in the stream at the same time; when one group arrived, the other would leave. Black people were not permitted to eat at "white" restaurants or lunch counters, or try on clothes in department stores, or ride in the front seats of buses or trains. White store clerks would not touch Black people's hands as they exchanged money in stores. There are numerous examples of the kind of humiliation Black people faced every day.

Possibly worst of all, white supremacists expected Black people to kowtow to them. It was considered an act of defiance for Black people to look white people straight in the eyes. If a white person and a Black person passed each other on the sidewalk, the Black person was expected to step off into the street. And Black people were not expected to "talk back" to white people. These practices were often backed up by the full force of local law-enforcement personnel. A prominent white person could have any Black person arrested for disobeying one of these unwritten "laws." White supremacists also used violence, as well as fear and intimidation tactics, such as burning down houses, to keep Black people "in their place." In many cases, this system worked because Black sharecroppers lived on land owned by whites and were dependent on the landowners, who were also the store owners and farm equipment suppliers, to keep a roof over their heads and food on their tables.

It is clear throughout these novels that part of Lorenz Graham's belief that "people are people" was the conviction that, in any group and under any social system, there are people with good hearts and the courage to treat others with kindness and dignity, even if doing so puts themselves at risk. And so, even though many of the white characters in these novels are bad actors, there are also white characters who do the right thing and who befriend or defend the Williams family in times of crisis. And, Graham makes clear, there are Black people who are bad actors as well.

The second and third novels in the series are set in the North. In *North Town*, David and his family have moved, in part because they had been so victimized in South Town that David's father could no longer make a living, and in part so that David could have access to an education that would better prepare him for medical school. His ambition is to become a physician and return to South Town to serve the people there. *Whose Town?* chronicles the Williams's second year in the North, when David is a senior in high school. (Although *South Town* appears to be set in the mid-1950s, and *Whose Town?* is supposedly two years beyond their move to the North, there appears to be some discrepancy in actual time setting. In *Whose Town?*, for example, Graham mentions the assassination of Dr. Martin Luther King, which took place in 1968, the year before *Whose Town?* was published. By moving the time forward, Graham is able to weave a more dramatic, and at the time more contemporary, backdrop into the stories.)

The two North Town books provide a picture of some of the

complexities of living in the North, and in large cities generally, in the late 1950s and 1960s. Although the social conditions in the North were not as bad for African Americans as they were in the South, and although the schools were not legally segregated by race, there were still bigotry and racism to contend with. All over America, African Americans were standing up in an organized way to demand social justice. In the South, the Civil Rights Movement was in full swing. In December 1955, Mrs. Rosa Parks's refusal to give up her seat on a bus had sparked the Montgomery, Alabama, bus boycott, and the rise to prominence of Dr. Martin Luther King, Jr. Dr. King and his followers preached nonviolence as a way to confront unjust conditions and to bring about change. Marches, sit-ins, and freedom rides challenged Jim Crow laws all over the South. In 1963, there was a massive March on Washington for Jobs and Freedom. "We Shall Overcome" became the anthem of the Civil Rights Movement.

Not everyone agreed that nonviolence was the best strategy for addressing African Americans' grievances. Many African Americans thought that people should protect their rights "by any means necessary." Sometimes actions were not organized, but exploded out of frustration with particular incidents or in response to conditions that simply became unbearable. In such cities as Los Angeles in 1965 and Detroit in 1967, some African Americans set fires and looted stores in their own neighborhoods out of frustration and rage. Not surprisingly, within African American communities there was often debate over how best to right the wrongs that African Americans had suffered for so long. The two North Town novels explore the range of attitudes and behaviors that were prevalent among both Black and white citizens, and place David and his family in positions that force them to grapple with the issues and decide what is the right thing for them to do; the right way for them to behave.

In the final book of the series, *Return to South Town*, David is completing his medical training and is fulfilling his dream of returning to his home town to set up practice in the community. The South has changed dramatically, but some of the people he knew when he was a teenager in South Town are still there, and their attitudes have not changed. Nevertheless, in the New South David finds friends, both Black and white, who are willing and able to help him overcome obstacles, and who bring home to him once again the fact that "people are people."

In many ways, Lorenz Graham was a pioneer. When the first three of his Town novels were published, there were very few honest, realistic books for young people about African American families. In that regard, Graham helped to pave the way for the development of contemporary African American literature for children and young adults. It was not easy to be a pioneer. If he had had his way, *South Town* would have been published years earlier. Even though it was based on his experiences living and working in Virginia, it took years for him to convince a publisher that his African American characters were true to life. But he persevered and refused to compromise the truth as he knew it. The books were pioneering, too, in their confrontation of the racist practices he knew existed in communities all over the nation.

It seems especially fitting that I complete this foreword on the one hundred and first anniversary of Lorenz Graham's birth. (He was born on January 27, 1902.) I had the privilege of meeting him on a couple of occasions, and he impressed me as a kind and gentle man with immense inner strength. The sincerity and depth of his belief in the ultimate triumph of social justice shines through his novels even today, more than forty years after the first one was published. He has left a priceless legacy, and it is my hope that these novels will provoke a new generation of readers to consider the authenticity of Graham's belief that "people are people," and the ways our world might change if we all acted on that belief.

Rudine Sims Bishop
Professor Emerita
The Ohio State University

Whose Town?

One

MR. WILLIAMS WAS LATE GETTING HOME that day. It was a Friday evening in February; Friday was payday. Mrs. Williams had tried to hold dinner for him, thinking that he might be just a little late.

"David, you and Betty Jane might as well eat," she said finally. "It's long after six o'clock, and I guess your pa won't be coming until later on. I'll wait for him."

"Oh, that's all right," Betty Jane said. "I'm not hungry. We can wait, too. Pa won't be too long coming, I know."

"You don't know how long he'll be," David protested. "I'm hungry, and besides I've got to go over to Carver for a meeting tonight."

"Just come on now," his mother said. Filling two plates with food, she placed them on the kitchen table. "You might as well both eat and get it over with. Your Pa might have stopped off with somebody, or maybe he's working overtime tonight."

"I don't think he's working overtime," David said. "They're short of work out there already. Nobody's working overtime."

The food looked good, and David started to eat at once.

"You didn't ask the blessing," Betty Jane said.

David bowed his head and closed his eyes and said a few words.

"That's asking the blessing?" Betty Jane demanded. "I couldn't even hear you."

"I wasn't talking to you," David said.

It was a good dinner, and David was hungry. They said he hadn't gotten his growth yet, although he had turned eighteen and he was over six feet tall, taller already than his father. He was built like Mr. Williams though, not so much heavy as wide in the shoulders, with long, powerful hands. It was his hands and the way he used them that marked him out as a football end.

Twelve-year-old Betty Jane was more like their mother; she would never be tall. Mrs. Williams was stout and light brown in color. She wore her hair brushed back, smooth and glossy, fastened in a knot at the back of her neck. She lived only for her family. Especially since they moved to North Town from the long familiar rural South, she had devoted herself almost entirely to the lives of her husband and children. David, she admired and looked at with adoring eyes, so tall, so manlike, so able to get along in the world of school and athletics with white people.

Betty Jane, who had said she was not hungry, ate heartily. When David teased her about going back for seconds, she said, "When I said I wasn't hungry, I didn't know it was going to be kidney stew and rice."

After David finished eating, he went into the living room and turned on the television. There was nothing particular that he wanted to see, but he was waiting for his father to come home. He wanted to use the car to drive over to the east side. The Williamses had talked above David's getting a car of his own, but he knew they couldn't afford it. Besides, his father knew he was a good driver and he allowed David to use the family car whenever he himself did not need it.

When he heard the sound of the car in the driveway, David got up and put on his sweater. The day had been chilly. There was no snow, but tonight would be really cold. Mr. Williams did not come in at once, and David turned back to the kitchen where Mrs. Williams was preparing to serve her second dinner.

"I'm going now, Ma," he said.

"Will you be late?" Mrs. Williams asked.

Although David answered, Mrs. Williams seemed no longer to be listening. The question was just a habit she had, a way of suggesting that David should not be late in returning.

It was a quarter of eight, and David should have already started for the Carver Community Center. He did not wait for his father to come into the house. Walking out the front door to the wide porch, he saw his father still seated behind the wheel of the car parked in the driveway.

As David approached, Mr. Williams turned toward him and opened the door. "I'm coming now, son," he said.

"I don't want to rush you," David said. "But I did want to go over to that meeting at Carver tonight."

"Meeting?" David's father stepped forward. "It's not going to be one of those Black Muslim meetings? I told you I don't want you to get mixed up in that kind of thing."

"Oh, I'm not mixed up in it." David was shaking his head as he moved toward the driver's side of the car. "Besides, this Moshombo's not a Muslim. He's a preacher. I just want to hear what he has to say."

"Davey boy," Mr. Williams said. "Whether he's a Muslim or not don't make any difference, but he really is one of those haters. He's only making trouble and asking for more trouble. He's out to get folks all stirred up. I don't like it."

"I know, Pa. And I don't expect to agree with everything he says." David turned the key, and the motor started its smooth hum. "Still, you've got to listen to every side, and then make up your own mind. That's what you've always said."

"Well, listen, but don't let them suck you in." David's father stepped away from the car as it moved slowly backward. "Just be careful," he called. "That's all. Just be careful."

David knew that he would be late, but he did not hurry as he drove toward the east side. The Williams family had lived there two and a half years ago, when they first came from the South. They had lived in an apartment on East Sixth Street, which in some ways was an improvement over what they had left behind. Down South, they had not had any plumbing, but they had lived in their own home. David had felt he was just about getting used to living in an apartment when his father found a two-story brick house on West Twenty-fourth Street for sale on excellent terms. The price was low, and Mr. Williams had enough savings to make the down payment. It was in a neighborhood on the west side where white people were moving out as colored buyers moved in.

Once the Williams family left the east side, David really began to understand how bad that section was. It was referred to by whites as a slum area, but colored people called it a ghetto. Many who lived there spoke of it with contempt and complained that the city failed to provide services such as lighting, police protection, street cleaning, and building inspection. Landlords could charge anything they wanted to in the way of rent, but they were not required to keep the buildings in good condition. Although the Tenth Street Elementary School, to which Betty Jane had gone, was not really a segregated school, most of the families in the area were colored. White families who lived on the east side sent their children across town to school.

David turned north on Main Street. The traffic this evening was light. Few people were on the streets, but most of the store windows were brightly lighted. At Sixth Street he made a right turn and passed the building where he and his family had lived when they first came to North Town. It was made of wood, one of several that stood in a row. All of them were badly in need of paint.

The one that he had lived in looked especially neglected. Beyond that block he passed a row of one-family houses. Some of them were very well kept. He had been told that most of them were owned by the families who lived in them. At Franklin Street he turned north again to approach the Carver Community Center.

He knew he was late in arriving, but he had not expected to find so many people and so many cars, particularly not so many police cars, as he saw. He had to squeeze by two of them, double parked in front of the center, and drive on to the next block before he could find a place to park. As he walked toward the building, he could hear the sound of music coming from the loudspeaker mounted outside the door. Other latecomers were hurrying with him as he walked quickly up the steps.

The meeting was being held in the gymnasium, which doubled as auditorium. At the platform end the hinged backboard for basketball had been removed from its place. Sections of collapsible bleachers had been set up around the walls, in addition to the folding chairs in the center of the floor. Every seat was taken. David tried to work his way forward past those who were standing in back. A male chorus, standing near the front, was singing. As the music ended, there was loud applause.

On the platform a man rose and stepped forward to the speaker's stand. Speaking through a microphone, he gave a short talk, emphasizing the fact that the people of North Town had been called together to hear a new leader. Describing him as a Moses in the land of Egypt crying out to his oppressor, "Let my people go!" he pronounced the name of the Reverend Prempey Moshombo.

Immediately a loud chord sounded on the piano. Those seated on the platform jumped to their feet and stood erect. The man who had been introducing the Reverend Moshombo motioned for everyone to stand. The piano continued with a few strains of martial music. It was impressive, but David did not recognize it as anything with which he was familiar. About a dozen people—both men and women—were on the platform. Now in their center there stood a tall black man, wearing a long white robe. Two other men stood like guards on his left and right. Both of them, also, wore robes, but their robes were striped in blue and white. The man in the center was the tallest of the three and the darkest in color. He wore his hair long, so that it gave the appearance of a black knitted cap. The two other men had their hair cut so short their heads might have been shaved. On the front, in the center of each of the robes was a large disklike emblem. On a field of white a clenched black hand was raised.

After the short burst of music, the tall man, the Reverend Moshombo, stepped forward to the microphone and raised his clenched fist. The people applauded. He turned from side to side as though seeking everyone's approval.

David did not know why, but he joined in the applause.

The Reverend Moshombo's speech could not have been called a sermon, but he delivered it as though he were preaching. He spoke with a foreign accent in a high-pitched voice. At first David found him hard to understand. He leaned forward, straining to catch the words.

Moshombo started by expressing pleasure at the number of brothers and sisters who had come to hear him. He thanked the local North Town committee. He announced that this was only one in a series of meetings being held throughout the nation, meetings that were daily becoming larger and more significant. In time—and this, he said, was a prophecy—in time all the black people in the city, the state, the nation, and the world would unite in the Brotherhood. They would move forward and upward in a mighty sweep that would restore to the black man the glory that had once been his in Ethiopia.

With this prophecy he drew another burst of applause.

As David listened, he felt sure that this man was not speaking of hate. All he was saying was that colored people should get together, that they should work for the benefit of one another, eliminating competition and strife, adopting a common goal for the welfare of all. Like other preachers, he urged the people to maintain lives of thrift and sobriety. Again and again the audience interrupted him with applause.

A pad and pencil were pushed toward David. On it there were three columns headed name, address, occupation. All those present were being asked to sign; David wrote down his name and address and his occupation, "Student."

Toward the close of his speech the Reverend Moshombo became emotional. He spoke of the three centuries of wrong inflicted upon "our people" shackled by the chains of slavery, dragged from their peaceful motherland, transported in the stinking holds of ships to a new land, where they were forced to till the soil and hew the wood and draw the water to enrich the white man. He spoke of babies being torn from the arms of their mothers so that they might be sold down the river and of young women being used as animals to satisfy the passions of their masters. He described a nation broken on the rack of civil war because the white man was unwilling to give up his ungodly gains, and he described the white man as still being unwilling to recognize the God-given rights of the black man. He said that the black man was still denied a chance to advance through fair employment, that he continued to be the last hired and the first fired, that the children of black people were given the shabbiest education, education designed not to elevate but to degrade. The black man's toil had built the white man's country, and the white man still wanted the black man to do the white man's will, to accept status as an inferior being, in the North as well as in the South, to be meek and humble like Uncle Tom of slavery days, to be exploited for his labor and for the wages that he must spend on slum rental, on spoiled groceries and rotten meat.

"For the first two hundred years in this wide land," he cried, "we were victims of the greed and the cruelty of the white man. We toiled for him in his fields and barns; we served him in his household, and the white man, our master, used his white power to lash our black backs as we chopped his cotton and toted his loads.

"Then there was emancipation, and the white man said the black man was free, but it wasn't long—no, it wasn't long—before white power took over again. Some of the white power was in the sheets of the Ku Klux Klan, but that wasn't the only place. There was white power in the black robes of the judges and the broadcloth of the lawmakers. There was white power in the vaults of the banks, and it sat with the directors and the managers of business establishments. The white man used white power to put up signs that said, 'White Only,' and to make our young men fight wars in foreign lands, where many a black skin was torn open in battle and black men died in the name of freedom and democracy, the likes of which they had never known."

As he drew toward the final shouting of his complaints, the people more and more cried out in approval of his words.

"Now, at long last, the black man is beginning to understand that just as there is white power, there is also black power, and while white power has held the black man down and kept him enslaved, his own God-given black power can lift him up and free him. The white man has laughed to see the black man divided into many parts, with the Baptists fighting against the Methodists, and the Baptists and Methodists fighting against the Catholics, and all the Christians fighting against the sinners. The rich black man has scorned the poor; the educated has looked down on the ignorant; the strong has turned his back on the weak. But a new day is dawning.

"We will take up this black power; together we will use it. Saint and sinner, rich and poor, North and South, in the bonds of the black brotherhood we will be united."

David was swept along emotionally with the rest of the crowd. He knew there was truth in what was being said. It could not be denied. He, too, wanted to see things made better for all black people. He was not sure how that goal would be reached, but the Reverend Moshombo spoke of united action. Well, David reasoned, if all the colored people could get together on some kind of program—all Negroes, North and South, rich and poor, educated and uneducated, skilled and unskilled, maybe even all the black people all over the world—surely if they could all get together in agreement, almost any goal could be achieved.

Looking around the auditorium, David was unable to see any of his own friends. There were several older people whom he had seen at church—perhaps they were even friends of his parents—but they were not people he knew well. He also recognized a number of the younger men: some he had seen at the Carver Community Center, and some he had known at school. After the main speech the man who acted as chairman called on a well-dressed man whom he introduced as the Honorable John Smith of Chicago. He made a plea for support and for financial assistance. This part, too, was reminiscent of church. A corps of ushers lined up across the front, then started through the crowd with metal pie plates. As they moved down the aisle, the male chorus sang; and as the ushers reassembled, the chorus broke into "We Shall Overcome," the song that had become the theme song of the civil rights movement.

Whenever David heard it sung, he thought of it as

being a different song from the one people used to sing down South. He could never understand how the tune became so changed. The way people sang it in South Town, it was like a marching song. The way he heard it sung in the North it was more like a funeral hymn.

The Reverend Moshombo, continuing in the spirit of a religious meeting, closed the meeting with a prayer. He was fiery and hopeful and demanding, but no one could say that he was expressing hatred.

As David moved out with the crowd, he heard his name called. Turning, he recognized an old acquaintance, John Henry Healey—or Head as he was generally called.

"What you say, man?" Head said as he pressed through the crowd. Coming closer, he grabbed David's hand. "Man, I thought that was you. I saw you when you first came in."

David expressed his pleasure at seeing Head. He said he had not realized he was in the crowd.

"Man, I was in the chorus, singing lead tenor with them," Head told him. "I'm working with the Reverend now, you know."

He went on to explain that the Reverend Moshombo had a staff that included musicians, a business manager, the two bodyguards who had been with him on the platform, and other workers.

"You got to give him credit," he said. "The Reverend Moshombo's doing a great work. Goes all over, holding big meetings and speaking all the time on radio and TV. He says what we got to do is get together and work as one. If the black man would only do that, he could get somewhere."

"Yes," David agreed. "I guess that's right."

Head went on to tell David what Moshombo's organization was going to do. The brotherhood would get jobs, decent jobs, for all its members. It would lend money to set up stores; it would open factories and bakeries and other food-processing plants.

"You can see the Reverend Moshombo's point," Head said. "The black man is spending his money now and making white business fat. Why can't he spend it in his own stores? What we got to do first is make the brotherhood strong."

Head walked with David to the car. He asked if David had a cigarette, and when David said he wasn't smoking, Head asked if Dave could make him a loan, maybe a dollar or a half dollar even.

He was very happy when David handed him a quarter and a dime, saying that was about all he had.

"Thanks, man," he said. "You'll be coming to the meetings. I'll see you there."

Head was one of the fellows who had dropped out of school to go to work. He lived with his mother who had been unable to do anything to help him. He was a naturally bright boy, smart in a way but not smart enough to get, much less hold, a job without a high school education and with no training or experience. Most of the time he was idle. David knew that Head had been "away" for nearly a year.

David drove home, looking forward to talking with his father about what the Reverend Moshombo had said. All he was urging on his listeners, it seemed, was the unity and strength that comes from being together. David could see truth in what he had heard. He was convinced there was nothing wrong in listening and accepting this man's thoughts. He expected his father to be interested. Perhaps Mr. Williams would ask him questions, trying to see where the speaker had been wrong in his argument. David recognized there was weakness in the presentation, but basically he thought that Moshombo had been altogether fair in what he had said.

At home no one asked David about the meeting. His father was sitting in the living room, and his mother was standing at the door leading into the hall. They evidently had been talking, for the TV was not on.

"David," Mrs. Williams said as she turned toward the kitchen, "you didn't have your dessert. Why don't you come and get it now?"

David followed his mother into the kitchen, although he would rather have stopped to tell his father about the meeting.

Betty Jane was at the kitchen table doing her homework. Some popular music was coming in on her transistor radio. She made room for David at the table. She looked at him without smiling and kept at her work. Mrs. Williams brought a piece of apple pie and a glass of milk, and then she stood watching him. David noticed that she, also, was very serious.

"What's the matter, Ma?" David asked finally.

"Your pa's been laid off," Mrs. Williams said. "Lots of the men were laid off today—maybe half of them. He says it may not be for long, but you can't tell."

No one asked David what he had heard at the community center. David himself forgot about it for a while. Mr. Williams had been working at the Foundation Iron and Machine Works for two and a half years. It was the only job he had ever had in North Town.

Being laid off wasn't like being out on strike. Foundation did contract work for the big auto manufacturers in Detroit and Dearborn. The strike was up there in Michigan. Because of cutbacks in those auto plants, the need for parts and supplies that Foundation turned out was diminished.

So it was that David's father, a first-rate machinist with less than three years' seniority, was laid off along with four thousand other workers.

"It ain't anything personal," Mr. Williams said. "It's not like they was trying to do something special to me. Just the same it's going to be hard. We were just about making out and getting our debts paid as it was. If they don't call me back soon, it will sure be hard."

TWO

ON SATURDAYS DAVID WORKED at a hardware store on South Main Street.

He liked his job. The hardware store and the other shops along the block served a community of private homes and small apartment houses. On Saturdays many home owners came in to purchase supplies and to secure advice about their painting and repair problems. Sam Silverman, the proprietor, seemed to have all the answers. Some of the clerks who had been in the business a long time could also give expert advice.

David was learning. He was beginning to be able to perform some of the services. He liked to help repair aluminum screens for windows and doors, but he was still not very skillful. He was learning to cut glass and with one swift stroke of the glass cutter to establish a line along which the sheet of glass would break when pressure was applied.

"Wait, wait," Sam Silverman called to him when he saw David was having trouble fitting a piece of glass. "I'll show you."

Sam cleared the worktable, took careful measurement, laid out a whole fresh sheet of glass, marked it, swept one stroke of the glass cutter, and broke the sheet evenly.

"It looks so easy when you do it," David said.

"Yes, I know, I know," Sam replied. "It's like everything else—easy when you know how. Now you don't know how, but you'll learn. It's easy when you know how *and* when you've had the practice. It takes both. I can show you how in a few minutes, but you'll have to practice to get your skill. Anybody can learn how to play the piano, but only with practice does it sound good, huh."

Sam was a man of small stature, thin and nervous, but filled with energy. He worked hard and expected his employees to do so, also. He would complain bitterly when any item was out of stock. He said that maintaining stock was the most important part of the hardware business. He had devised an elaborate system for checking inventory and for calling attention to shortages or an unusual demand in a specific item. He scolded his employees, but they liked him. They tried to meet his standards.

On the first day that David was employed, Sam Silverman said to him, "Just call me Sam. Everybody calls me Sam. Never mind the mister bit."

David had laughed and said, "All right, if that's the way you want it."

Just the same he still found it difficult to call this man, older than his own father, by his first name.

Sam had two white full-time clerks and a woman bookkeeper. The only other colored employee was an older man who drove the delivery truck, clerked, and helped in many ways. Like Sam, John Bowman seemed to know all the answers, and he was able to give useful advice to customers. He knew the merchandise. Whenever even an inexpensive item was out of stock, he could keep the customer satisfied by securing a satisfactory substitute and delivering it. David felt that of all the employees Sam must consider John Bowman the most valuable.

David had started to work in the hardware store during the Christmas rush. It was John Bowman who had spoken to him one day about staying on.

"You doing all right, boy," he said. "You catch on fast, and you don't mind working, do you?"

David said yes, that was true; he liked to work. Besides, he had had quite a bit of experience working in various places.

"Tell you what," John went on as though in confidence, "being as you're going to school, how about working around here part time, say Saturdays? I think old Sam could use you."

David thought about the football team, which would have ruled out any chance of his working on Saturdays if this were the fall, but now that the season was over and he was no longer going out for athletics, he would have time and he liked the job.

"That would be great," he said. "I'd like that. Do you

really think he would keep me on?"

"Well, don't say nothing about it," John said, still with his confidential air. "And especially if Sam says anything to you about it, don't let on that we talked."

It was when Sam handed David his pay at the end of the Christmas vacation period that he proposed that their relationship continue for at least one day a week, and perhaps extra days, if David were free. He would pay David by the hour. On Saturdays he could work ten hours.

This Saturday morning, just before eight o'clock, David and the rest of the staff were waiting in front of the hardware store when Sam drove up in the pickup truck. Everybody agreed that it was not going to rain and so they would have the outside display on the sidewalk. David put out a stack of galvanized garbage cans. Then Sam decided to have him add a stack of bright-colored plastic trash containers. David pushed out a wheelbarrow loaded with one- and five-gallon cans of paint for sale at reduced prices. He propped two aluminum stepladders near the doorway. Last of all, a bundle of chicken wire and a roll of roofing paper were added. David had to hurry. At eight o'clock on Saturday there were always one or two customers waiting and complaining that the store did not open early enough.

He helped to wait on the customers. As soon as there was some slack, Sam told him to bring some kegs of nails to refill the bins. David was kept more than busy. He made a sale of paint to a lady who doubted that the paint displayed at a special price was worth the money.

"Oh, yes," he told her, "that's a good paint, and the

regular price is what you see marked on the can. It's just a one-day special, but it's a really good paint. We recommend it."

"Never mind, boy," the woman replied. "I know about these sales. If it was any good, they wouldn't mark it down. Give me the other kind."

John Bowman had heard the conversation. As he walked by, he said under his breath so that only David could hear him, "Just like a spook."

Later in the morning he said to David, "Saw you at the meeting last night. The man was speaking the gospel truth, wasn't he?"

"Yeah, it sounded real good."

"I didn't know you'd be interested," John said. "You going to school, and all, and living on the west side."

"Well, I guess school and the west side can't change a man but just so much anyway." David told him.

"Ain't that the living truth!" John replied.

Just before noon he asked David what he was planning to do that day for lunch.

"Oh, I'll probably go down the street and get a couple of hamburgers. That's what I usually do," David replied.

"That ain't no food for a man," John said with a smile. "You come with me, and I'll show you where you can get some soul food. That's the kind of stuff that will stick to your ribs."

David agreed. He knew that John meant he would take him to a place where they would have old-fashioned Southern cooking. If he had not both liked and respected John, he would have told him that in his own home he almost always had soul food and that when he went out and paid for a meal he enjoyed having something different.

John took the pickup truck, and they quickly made their way over to East Tenth Street.

"It don't look like much," John said as they walked up the steps of a house that had a sign in the window advertising meals at all hours. "It don't look like much, but it's real home cooking, and they give you plenty for your money."

The place was scrupulously clean. Each of the tables was covered by oilcloth in a calico design. A very large woman in a white uniform called out a cheerful greeting as she recognized John Bowman. Others who were seated at the tables also seemed to know him. John and David sat down at one of the tables set for two. After some discussion they both ordered dinners of fried catfish, which the woman said had come in fresh that morning. The food was good. It was hot. There was an abundance of fish and a large dish of cabbage and boiled potatoes and a plate stacked with cornbread. The cornbread was the kind that had been fried on top of the stove rather than baked in the oven. It was truly "soul food."

As they ate, John turned the talk to the meeting with the Reverend Moshombo. He wanted to know just what David thought about what had been said.

"It sounds all right," David told him. "It sounds good if you could ever get all the colored people together to unite and go in one direction. It's just that I don't see how he plans to get that kind of agreement."

"Well, it's got to come. It's got to come, and you will see it." John said, striking the table with his fist to emphasize his words. "It's-got-to-come! The black man is eternally behind. He always comes out the small end of the horn. He's got nothing now—he's never had anything—but trouble and woe. He's got to wake up and see where his strength is."

"But don't you think, John, that things are getting better?" David was thinking of the conditions he had known in the South as compared with the conditions he saw around him in North Town. "Most colored people are working, and some of them are getting good pay. Lots of them are buying homes, and young people are going to school. We have more lawyers and doctors coming along all the time."

"But it ain't enough." John seemed very sure of this. "It ain't moving fast enough. Too many of our people got no jobs. Too many on relief, too many got nothing at all, and they got no chance to get anything, either. That's what the man was talking about, and he's right. What we have to do is to get together to make things better for everybody. Can't you see that?"

"Well now, take your own situation. Even take mine," David said. "We are both working for Sam Silverman. You got a full-time job, and I don't know what he pays you, but you're buying your own house, and your kids are going to school. My daddy works at the Foundation Iron and Machine plant. He's buying our house, too, and I'm going to school. That looks like progress to me. Progress for both of us."

"Progress? Progress?" John said. "How long is it going to take? It's been more than a hundred years since Lincoln freed the slaves. Your daddy and me and lots of other people just now started piling up debt to buy theirselves a little house. I say we deserve better than that. The white folks getting richer while we get more and more in debt. They own the town. They practically own us, too. So that's how it is, and we got to get together and change it."

The argument continued through the rest of the lunch hour. As they drove back to the store, John ended the discussion with an invitation.

"Now, look, Dave Williams," he said just before they reached the parking place at the back of the store. "You're young, and you're getting your schooling. That's fine. And you'll probably go on and get a good education and make something of yourself. You got to remember, though, that not everybody lives on the west side and not everybody gets the chance you got. I want you to see this thing clear. Tonight I'm going to another meeting, and I'd like you to go with me."

"Well, not tonight," David said. "I've got something else to do. But we'll talk about it some more."

Actually David felt that it was his own experience and viewpoint that needed to be explained to John Bowman. He knew there were some good points in what John, and others like him, said. Of course, progress wasn't fast enough, but David had an idea that such as it was it was steady. Furthermore he did not believe that any sudden changes could be made. He knew that education was a slow process, and he believed that education would solve many of the Negroes' problems. He was eager to talk about it. He believed that Negroes could solve their problems by hard work and right living and that education was their most valuable help. He thought he could prove it even to John Bowman.

It was true that he had something else to do that Saturday night. He had a date with Jeanette Lenoir. They were going to a party at Maybelle Reed's home.

He had hoped to use the car, but once again Mr. Williams did not come home until late. David waited as long as he could, then he left the house on foot. It was not far. He did not mind either the walking or the cold, but it wasn't so good when taking a girl out if you didn't have a car.

Jeanette must have been waiting for him. She opened the door almost before he had time to ring.

"Oh, Dave!" she exclaimed excitedly. "We're going to be late, and I promised to help Maybelle."

"Sorry about that. I was trying to wait for my dad to come home with the car. We'll have to walk. Do you mind?"

"Of course, I don't mind." Jeanette was smiling, obviously glad to see him. "Only," she added, "I'm sorry about my promise to Maybelle."

David noticed that she was wearing a short jacket.

"Maybe you'd better wear a coat," he said. "It's cold out tonight."

Jeanette went to the hall closet and took out a black winter coat with a fluffy white collar. Then she called up the stairway, "Mom, I'm taking your white tam. O.K.?"

Mrs. Lenoir gave her assent, and Jeanette was soon ready and out the door. She ran down the steps ahead of David and then turned to smile up at him. Her dark face seemed to float in the wide collar under the topping of the soft white cap. The porch light showed her happy smile and glinted in her large eyes.

David put his arms around her. "You look like something good to eat," he said, trying to place a kiss on her lips. It was not an altogether successful attempt, but he was glad that Jeanette did not turn away. He breathed deeply of her perfume, and as she turned, he realized it was not in rejection or displeasure. She simply made David understand that it was time to start walking.

They walked the three blocks to the Reed home with Jeanette's hand resting in the crook of David's arm. He liked the sound of the click of her heels. She was tall for a girl and slender. He had been told that they looked nice together. Six months younger than David, she had graduated from Central High School a year ahead of him and was now attending State College.

As they walked, she told him of incidents on the campus. He, in turn, told her something about his job at the hardware store—just little things. He wanted to talk to her about the speech he had heard, but they sometimes argued about black power, and he was not in the mood to try to solve the race problem tonight.

The party at the Reeds' was in honor of Maybelle's birthday. Many of the guests were already there when David and Jeanette arrived. David had the warm feeling that he knew almost everyone there and they all liked him, and that he and they were all about equally well dressed. He also liked the knowledge that his girl was one of the most popular, and that when she was dancing with other men, most of the other girls were glad to be dancing with him.

David had brought a gift for Maybelle, but the presents were not opened. Except for the birthday cards, no display was made. A tape stereo was playing in the living room, and most of the boys and girls were dancing. In the dining room, just across the wide hall, a large punch bowl surrounded by trays of small sandwiches and sliced cake formed another center of attraction. Mrs. Reed kept coming in from the kitchen with more sandwiches, with bottles of soda and boxes of sherbet to add to the punch.

Maybelle's father, Sergeant Reed, spent most of the evening in the back of the house. He was not wearing his uniform, but everyone there recognized him each time he passed through to greet or to say good-bye to relatives and friends. He and his fellow officers, some of them in uniform, stayed in the den. They had their smokes and refreshments back there, with the television set on and a basketball game to watch. At some parties on the west side there was danger from party crashers. These uninvited guests would refuse to leave, and often started fights. Sometimes they threw things, breaking up the furniture and smashing windows. Because everyone knew that Maybelle's father was a member of the police force there was never any such danger at her house.

People said that Maybelle was beautiful. She was light brown in color with long, naturally straight hair. Her eyes were large, and her teeth were beautifully even and pearly white. When she was excited, her long lashes fluttered above her big dark-brown eyes.

"Bet she practices that in the mirror every night," one of the girls had said.

Maybelle was vivacious, and David agreed she was altogether lovely, although he liked Jeanette far more. Sergeant Reed, the only colored sergeant on the local police force, treasured his daughter and guarded her carefully. His good salary enabled his family to live comfortably in one of the nicest homes occupied by colored people.

Promptly at one o'clock the last of Sergeant Reed's friends came through the front of the house from the den at the back. As they moved toward the front door, there were calls of "Good night," "Had a nice time," "See you next week," and other farewell remarks. At about the same time Mrs. Reed took the punch bowl off the table in the dining room. David heard one of the fellows say, "Looks like the party's over."

They had had their fun. It had been a good party, and just about everybody was ready to leave. Still, it was not late, and some of them—particularly some of the boys—wanted to have more fun before they went home. Jimmy Hicks had already promised David and Jeanette a ride. Jimmy, who was there with his girlfriend, Naomi, was also taking Alonzo Webster and his girlfriend, Gertrude Smith.

David went to the kitchen to say good-bye to Mrs. Reed. "We sure had a nice time," he told her.

"Well, I'm glad, son," Mrs. Reed said. "And it was nice of you to tell me so. Now, let me see. I forget names, though I always remember faces. I never forget a face, but what is your name?"

"My name is David, David Williams," David replied. "You haven't seen me too often before."

"Oh, yes. I've heard Maybelle and Jeanie talk about you. Well, now, David, you must come again soon."

By the time David got outside, the others were already getting into their cars, calling farewells and promises to meet. The heavy bass voice of Alonzo Webster—Lonnie as they all called him—was louder than anyone else's. Lonnie always talked like that; he sounded angry even when he was trying to be funny. Lonnie was not as tall as David, but he was heavier. He played guard on the football squad at North Central, but the coach seldom used him because Lonnie was always having trouble with other players on the team.

Jimmy Hicks was at the wheel of the Plymouth with Naomi in front. David and Jeanette got into the back seat with Lonnie and Gertrude. It was a tight fit, but nobody cared.

Presently David heard Jimmy say, "But I'm hungry. It wouldn't hurt to stop for just a little while."

Naomi said, "My folks know what time the Reeds' parties are over. They'll be looking for me."

Gertrude said, "Oh, Naomi, your folks are going to be asleep anyway by the time you get home. They won't know what time you come in."

"That's what you think." Naomi turned around to look back. "My mother never closes her eyes as long as I'm out of the house."

Lonnie said, "My mother gives me that line, too. I just tell her if she wants to stay awake and worry that's her business."

"Well, anyway," Gertrude said as she snuggled over toward Lonnie, "I'm hungry, and if anybody wants to go for burgers, I'm with it."

A few minutes later David realized that Jimmy was not taking Naomi home. He was going toward the Eastlake Turnpike, and when he reached it, he made the boulevard stop and turned left. Naomi fussed a little. Lonnie and Gertrude were very quiet. David had nothing to say. Jeanette carried her own key, so she was not worried about getting in late.

At a brightly lighted crossroad the white columns of the Plantation Drive-In stood out sharply on the horizon. Jimmy turned in and parked. David hurried to get out of the car.

"O.K.," he said. "Name it."

Everybody wanted burgers; nobody wanted onions. The five in the car wanted Cokes, and David decided he would have coffee. Among the crowd of customers inside the glass enclosure, David recognized a boy from Central.

When David said, "Hi," the fellow only nodded and turned his back to talk with his friends. David wasn't bothered. After all the guy was not a friend of his, only someone who went to the same school.

He got his order, paid for it, and started off with the bag of hamburgers and french fries and the tray of five Cokes and one hot coffee. As he moved toward the door, he was bumped. He knew it was deliberately done.

"Hey, black boy, watch where you're going." The speaker was a young man, probably in his early twenties. He was not as tall as David, but he was certainly heavier.

David was aware that everybody in the place was looking at him, and he said, "I am watching, and I know where I'm going."

"Yeah, he thinks he's smart," someone else said.

"So it looks like you need a little help." It was the fellow who had bumped him who said that. At the same moment David was pushed from behind to collide with the agitator, who struck out with his fist at David's face.

It was only a glancing blow, but David's head went back and he dropped the food and drinks. That was the first of many blows from all sides. The counterman began shouting at the crowd: "Take it outside. Take it outside. Don't start that stuff in here. Take it outside."

David was not afraid. He was used to hard physical conflict, and he was in good shape. He swung hard with his fists and made each blow tell. Only one or two of the white boys came at him; the rest stayed out of reach, but they were hurling sugar containers, catsup bottles, and other troublesome missiles. David got his first attacker and another fellow about his own age on the same side of him, and he waded in. He knew he could have run off and left them all, but the food he had paid for was scattered on the floor. He had been attacked unfairly, and he was angry.

Behind him the doors opened from the outside, and Jimmy Hicks and Lonnie Webster rushed in. The white boys in the crowd went out the door on the opposite side and ran for their cars. The counterman was shouting into the telephone. David and his friends turned and ran for their car.

Jimmy Hicks put the car into reverse; the tires spun on the pavement as he backed and then swung onto the road, headed toward town.

He drove at high speed on the turnpike. Behind him two cars followed from the Plantation parking lot. As they approached Broadway, they saw a police car with its red domelight flashing, coming from the city.

"It's the cops," David said. "We'd better stop and tell them."

"We can't stop," Jimmy said. "The whites will be on us, and it will be the cops and the paddies against us."

The Plymouth passed the police car going in the opposite direction. David looked back and saw the police car brake to a swift stop, back and wheel, and come on again, following behind them.

"Hold it, Jimmy. Hold it," David called. "You'll just make it worse for all of us. Hold it. We'll tell them."

By this time they were not too far out of town. Jimmy saw an all-night service station. He braked hard; the tires screamed. Jimmy turned in and stopped. The two cars that had been following went by the turn. The police car swung in behind the Plymouth, turning almost over on two wheels.

Two officers got out, carrying guns—the one from the right side with a shotgun, the other with a revolver.

"Come out with your hands up," David heard. "All of you, I mean."

The boys got out first and turned to help the girls.

"Keep your hands up, I said," commanded the officer with the shotgun.

There was nothing else to do.

"Over by the wall. Keep your hands up. Line up. Lean against the wall. All right now. One phony move, and you're going to get it. Don't forget we got you covered."

One of the officers came down the line, making a search. He patted down the bodies of each of the boys, then passed his hands over the bodies of the girls. The two cars that had gone by the gas station returned. Another squad car pulled in, with siren screaming.

David, still facing the wall, with his hands thrust high above his head heard someone say, "That's them all right. That big black one jumped me."

"That big black one there," the voice continued. "He's the one that attacked me. But all of them was in it. The girls, too."

By glancing sideways, David could see Jeanette and Naomi and Gertrude. Jeanette and Naomi were handcuffed together; Gertrude was alone, her hands fastened together in front of her. The girls were hustled into one of the squad cars. Then Jimmy Hicks and Lonnie Webster were handcuffed together, and last, David's own hands were fastened in a sort of chain device, which was drawn very tight, cutting into his flesh.

One of the officers asked who had been driving. When Jimmy said that he had, his handcuffs were unfastened while he got out his driver's license. Then he was told to move the car to the back of the parking area, where he locked it up. They let him keep the key.

The boys said nothing as they rode downtown. David realized that because he was eighteen he would be separated from the others, who would be treated as juveniles.

"Look," he said while they walked up the steps at police headquarters, "we'd better get a phone call to Sergeant Reed. He'll know what to do."

When they stood in the front room before the desk sergeant, they still had not seen the girls. They had not seen them, but they could hear the voice of Naomi, who was off in another room down the hall.

"What am I being arrested for?" she was asking, crying almost hysterically. "What am I being arrested for? I haven't done anything."

At the desk an officer listed the boys' names, ages, and addresses. Something was said about being held on suspicion of assault. David was told to empty his pockets. His billfold, with his driver's license and identification cards and his money, $12.30 in all, were put into an envelope, and he was given a receipt. He was led down the hall away from the others and then down a flight of stairs. Without a word the officer opened a door of white metal bars covered by a heavy screen. David stepped through the opening, and the door clanged shut behind him.

He was alone in a large room with one high window, barred and screened like the door. The benches that stretched along two sides of the room were firmly attached to the wall. David sat down on one of them and tried to think of what he might do. He was not too concerned about himself. He thought that at a trial he could prove he was innocent of any wrong. He was worried about the girls, though. He feared they might be held until morning. He knew that Jeanette would understand, but Mr. Lenoir would be harsh. He would say that they should have gone directly home after the party. Naomi's mother, pacing the floor, would be wondering where her poor child was.

David did not have long to wait. The officer who had locked him up came back and, with loud clanking, unlocked the barred door. He ordered him out and led him back upstairs, turning in at a door marked Juvenile Bureau. Sergeant Reed was there, in his uniform. Another man, a white man, not in uniform, sat behind the desk. Jeanette, Naomi, and Gertrude were seated in front of the desk, Jimmy Hicks and Lonnie Webster standing behind them.

The man at the desk spoke to David first, asking if he were David Andrew Williams and if he were eighteen years of age. When David had answered him, the man spoke again.

"You'll understand that your situation is a little different from these others," he said. "Just the same you have your constitutional right to answer questions or to remain silent. You also have the right to a lawyer, and if you cannot afford to employ one, a lawyer will be provided for you. And you must understand that anything you may say can be used as evidence and held against you."

After David agreed that he understood, Sergeant Reed spoke.

"Williams, I want you to understand this very clearly," he said, walking over toward David. "The juvenile officer is making an investigation of this matter. We have told him that all of you young people were at my house earlier. Hicks here has said that the six of you went by the Plantation for hamburgers and that you went inside the place and that's where the fight started. Now you are not on trial, but do you want to tell us what happened?"

David told them.

The juvenile officer looked at Sergeant Reed and said, "I can't see any reason why we should hold these juveniles at all. Maybe those other people will want to bring charges against Williams here, but I'm certainly willing to let the others go. Their parents can come and pick them up anytime."

"Now, look, these kids were guests in my home," Sergeant Reed said. "They are not delinquents. I know David Williams, too. He's no hoodlum. You can release all the kids to me, and I'll take them home myself."

David's heart sank. Then he felt better as he heard Sergeant Reed add, "I'll go out here and see about Williams, too. He won't be any trouble." He turned toward David and said, "You come with me."

It took only a few minutes of conversation between Sergeant Reed and the desk sergeant. David was handed the envelope with his personal property. He checked it out while the sergeant watched, acknowledging that everything was there.

Silently Sergeant Reed led all six of them to his car in the parking lot. No one spoke.

Jeanette got in the front seat, and David got in after her. He put his arm around her. She was trembling. He held her close, trying to comfort her, trying to make her feel that she was safe.

"Of course, you all know," Sergeant Reed said once the car was underway, "none of this would have happened if you folks had gone home after the party. What's the matter with you? Wasn't there enough to eat at my house? You got to go out early Sunday morning and get some breakfast before you go home? Huh?"

"But we didn't start anything, Sergeant Reed," Lonnie Webster said. "From where we were sitting in the car, we could see everything that happened. You know that the drive-in's got an all-glass front. David Williams didn't start the fight. He didn't attack anyone."

The others agreed, especially the girls.

"I believe you," the sergeant said. "You don't have to convince me. Just the same it wouldn't have happened if you had gone home the way you should have. If those whites press charges, they can make it look bad, especially for Williams."

The sergeant had not asked them for directions or said to which house he would go first. David realized that he was driving them back to the service station where they had left Jimmy Hicks's car. As he pulled in to the parking lot, they saw that the night attendant was sweeping near the car.

The car was still where Jimmy had parked it, but as they drew nearer they saw that the windows had been broken. Glass was scattered all over the pavement. Jimmy jumped from the car. Sergeant Reed walked over to the attendant. "What's been going on here?" he demanded.

"I don't know. I was sitting in the office. The car was out here. I heard some noise, and when I came out, this is what I seen," the attendant said.

"You must have seen who did it," David said. "You don't have to lie to us, man."

"Ain't lying. I didn't see nothing. I just heard something. I don't know who done it."

Jimmy had the keys, but he could not drive the car. Windshield, windows, lights, everything made of glass, had been shattered. It must have taken some time to finish such a job, even with several people working at it.

Jimmy wanted to telephone to his home, but Sergeant Reed said it would be better to call a wrecker and have the car towed away to a repair shop. At least, it would be safe there and it would be better than having to post a guard for it here.

"Besides," he said. "this will be an insurance matter. I'll explain it later to your folks."

It did not take long for the wrecker to arrive after the sergeant put in a telephone call.

They took Gertrude home first. Sergeant Reed went to the door with her. Mr. and Mrs. Smith invited him inside, and the sergeant went in to explain what had happened. He came back to the car without speaking and drove to Naomi's house.

Here the porch light was on, and from the car they could see that lights were on all over the house, upstairs and down. Naomi was crying by the time she got out of the car. The door opened before the sergeant and Naomi reached the steps. Both Naomi's parents were there. They ran out, asking questions. Naomi began crying harder, and there was a big fuss. Again Sergeant Reed went into the house; he remained there longer than he had at Gertrude's home.

David could feel that the trembling had left Jeanette's body, but he kept his arms around her. He told himself that she was leaning on him for strength.

"I never thought, I never even dreamed," she said, "that I would ever be arrested."

"But you weren't really," David protested. "You haven't done anything. There are no charges against you."

"Not arrested?" She sat up and turned to look at David. "Handcuffed? Handled by those white men? Taken to jail?" With a sob she covered her face with her hands. "I feel so dirty."

She would not be comforted. David tried to talk to her, but she seemed not to hear his soft words or the angry voices of Jimmy and Alonzo in the back seat.

At her home she thanked Sergeant Reed and told him that he need not bother about her further. She had her key; her parents would not be concerned. David would walk with her to the door.

When he came back to the car, David heard the sergeant say as he turned on the switch, "Parents can sure get hurt bad."

They drove to Lonnie Webster's and then to lower Main Street to let Jimmy Hicks out. Sergeant Reed went in to explain about the car. When he returned and began driving toward David's house, the sergeant seemed more willing to talk.

"You know, Williams," he began, "I can believe everything that you say. I know how some of these whites are. Without a uniform on, it could happen to me. But that's just why I advise you young people to avoid contact with these toughs as much as you can. At one and two o'clock in the morning, especially on Saturday night and Sunday morning, they get rough. Those of them that are out have probably been drinking. They may be high on pot or pills or this LSD stuff. They're dangerous, and when you go out among them, it's like walking through a field with rattlesnakes in the grass. Except they don't give you any warning before they strike—maybe they're more like cottonmouth moccasins. They're real dangerous, and they can hurt you bad. Not much use talking about rights when you're hurt. You got a right to walk through the field, too, but if the snakes are out there, you can get killed."

The sergeant went on talking. David did not speak until he was nearly home; then he asked him for advice. "What do you think I ought to do now that I'm in it, Sergeant Reed?"

The officer drove on for a while before he spoke. "If those buggers file a complaint and then follow it up, you'd better get a lawyer. Maybe it won't come to that, but you never can tell."

As they pulled up in front of David's house, the sergeant added, "I don't know your folks, Williams, but you tell them that if I can help at all, they should call me."

THREE

DAVID DID NOT AT ONCE TELL HIS PARENTS about his arrest. It was not that he was trying to keep it from them. He knew that eventually they would have to know.

On Sunday morning when he got up, the others were going to church.

"Don't think I can make it," he said. "I've got some studying to do."

"Yeah. What time did you come in last night?" Betty Jane asked with a sly smile.

David did not answer, and the question was not pursued. His mother told him he could get his own breakfast: the sausage was cooked; the batter for hotcakes was ready in a bowl.

He was still in his pajamas when the others left, and

before he dressed, he made his breakfast. Just as he was sitting down to eat, the phone rang. It was Jimmy Hicks.

Jimmy's mother was very upset about the car. Jimmy wanted David to speak to her.

"Jimmy says you started the fight," David heard Mrs. Hicks say. Her voice was harsh over the telephone. "So you can just tell your folks that I'm going to hold them responsible for the damages."

She went on to say that she did not allow Jimmy to run around at night. He knew he was to use the car only to go to the party; she was sure he would never have gone out on the road unless others had persuaded him. She just wasn't going to put up with that kind of thing.

David tried to get a few words in edgewise, but he knew that Mrs. Hicks was not listening to anything he said. Finally he told her he would come over to her house to talk about it.

At any other time David would have enjoyed his breakfast. On Sunday mornings he often ate alone. Today he was worried. He would have to tell his father. He hoped he would have a chance to talk to him and explain before other people told him about the trouble.

David knew that his father was a reasonable man. They had always understood each other better than most fathers and sons. For several months Mr. Williams had been sick and unable to work. It had been when David was seventeen, and he had worked and helped his mother as though he were head of the house. After his recovery Mr. Williams had looked upon his son with even greater confidence and trust. He had shown his pride in David's development as a football player. He had expressed high hopes for David's future and promised to help all he could as David continued his education.

Although he would have said that his father was a real good guy, understanding and helpful, David hated to tell him about his arrest. It would be one more thing to worry him.

Jimmy Hicks lived with his mother and his younger brothers and sisters on lower Main Street, on the second floor of a four-story brick apartment house.

In response to David's knock, the door was opened a few inches held by a safety chain. Then Jimmy recognized David and let him in.

"She's in there," he said, nodding toward the front of the apartment.

David followed Jimmy up the narrow hall to the front room. Mrs. Hicks was lying on the couch, holding a baby, who might have been two years of age, in her arms. Three other children, younger than Jimmy and older than the baby, were also in the room. The television set was on. It was on loud, but no one seemed to be paying any attention to it. It was just there.

Mrs. Hicks sat up as David entered. She was wearing red slacks. Her feet were bare, but there was a pair of high-heeled gold slippers on the floor. She pushed her feet into them.

"You're David Williams, huh?" she began. "You must be lots older than Jimmy." David said he was about a year older, having turned eighteen.

"Well, you should have known better. I blame you. You should have known better. Bad enough to go riding around with some girls after a party, but then going in there and getting in a fight with some white folks, and getting yourself arrested, and getting my car all smashed up! You should have known better," Mrs. Hicks said. She stopped to get out a cigarette and light it.

David tried to argue with her. "Now look, Mrs. Hicks," he said, "it wasn't my idea that we go for a ride. And when we got to the Plantation, the only reason I went in was that I had some money and I was going to pay for everything. They jumped me. I didn't start anything, and I couldn't help myself."

"You had no business going there in the first place." Mrs. Hicks stood up, putting the baby down on the couch behind her. "You had no business going there in the first place. You knew that was white folks' place, and white folks play on Saturday night just like colored folks. And you know it don't matter if they do call it North Town; it's the white folks' town just the same. If you all had to go someplace, why didn't you go over to the east side and find some barbecue joint?"

The baby started to cry. "I guess we just didn't think about it," David said.

"Yeah, that's the trouble. You didn't think." Mrs. Hicks put her hands on her hips. "Now the man's got my car, going to cost real hard money to get it back. I got no transportation. I got no money, and you and your folks are going to have to dig down and put up the cash. That's how it is."

"But you act like it was all my fault," David said.

"Well, it sure wasn't mine. And it was your fault. You

the oldest one. You the one went in the joint. You the one started swinging your fists. Trying to fight back at white folks. I don't know what's got into you young people."

Jimmy interrupted her. "My mom's got some of that old slave psychology in her," he said. "Tries to say that a black man shouldn't ever stand up to a white man. She goes for all this nonviolent stuff, too. I say that old turn-your-cheek stuff might've been all right in Bible days, but it don't work now. Man's got to stand up for his rights, no matter what color he is and no matter what color the guy is that hits you."

"Yes, and what do it get you?" Mrs. Hicks turned on her son. "What do it get you at all? Throwed in jail! My car smashed up! And who going to pay for it all? Your big two-fisted friend here, David Williams! He the one going to pay?"

"But you got to stand up to them, Ma," Jimmy said. "That's the trouble now. We been taking low too long. They think they can get away with anything. Your generation didn't fight back. But there's a new day coming. Dave Williams done right, and we're going to back him up."

"So you gonna back him up! So you gonna pay for my car?"

David knew that he had to say something more. He turned toward Mrs. Hicks. "Mrs. Hicks, you must understand this," he said. "I didn't start any fight, and there wasn't anything different I could have done. They jumped on me, and I had to protect myself."

"You could have run, couldn't you? You could have give them your backside and lit out."

David and Jimmy both spoke at the same time. David said, "No, I couldn't!" Jimmy said, "Not David Williams, he couldn't!"

"Then you are a fool!" Mrs. Hicks said. "But just because you're a fool, don't make no difference to me. You still going to have to pay for my car."

David could see he was getting nowhere. Jimmy expressed his sympathy and understanding, but David knew he was going to have to pay Mrs. Hicks something for the repair of the car or he would have a lot of trouble with her. Where the money would come from was another matter. He told Mrs. Hicks he would have to talk it over with his folks.

As he walked home, he asked himself if he had done wrong. No, he told himself. He had done the only thing there was to do. He had had to fight, and even if the blows hadn't come on him so fast and hard, he would have still had to defend himself.

He thought about Mrs. Hicks. She was a woman without a husband, who had grown up in the South and was convinced that walking humble before white folks, taking their insults, turning and running, "giving your backside" as she called it, were the best ways to deal with mean whites. Well, David had lived in the South most of his life. His father had taught him that you didn't always fight back, but on the other hand you didn't run away. Sometimes it was better to go down fighting than to give up altogether. And he had moved his family out of the South in order to try to find a place where a man could stand as a man, in spite of his dark skin.

Even in the North the Williams family had had some

rough experiences. David had run into problems at Central High School. Now as he looked back, he figured he had learned you must keep going forward, no matter what happened. He had learned that all white people weren't against colored people. In fact, he had found that white people weren't very different from colored people. Some of them were decent; some were no good at all; the majority lay somewhere in between. Black folk, white folk, and he supposed, red folk and yellow folk, too, would fall into the same kind of classification.

One thing seemed certain; when there was trouble—like on Saturday night—white people stayed together, and colored people did the same.

When David got home, his family were already at dinner. He joined them at the table. He wanted to discuss his troubles with his father, but Mr. Williams had already started on the subject of the layoff.

"Like the man says, when Foundation lays off four thousand hands, the whole town feels it."

"But they'll be getting unemployment insurance, won't they?" David thought that he should try to add a cheery note.

"So a man's been making $120 a week, and now he comes down to maybe $50 or $60," his father said. "He can't meet his bills and feed his family on that."

"Well, maybe it won't be for long," Mrs. Williams said.

"You never can tell about this kind of thing," Mr. Williams said. "Could be two, three, weeks—could be that many months. You just can't tell."

"Well, David can get another night job," Betty Jane

suggested. "He likes to work at night, and besides, he made good money before when he was working at Foundation."

Mr. Williams snorted. "When they're laying off men, they're not about to hire boys. You can count on that," he said.

As soon as he was through eating, Mr. Williams pushed back his chair, saying he had to go across town. Again David was disappointed. He did not know when he would be able to talk with his father.

He called Jeanette.

"I've just got to study," she said. "I'm way behind in my outside reading, and I don't even have the books. I may have to go to the library."

David, too, had studying to do, but he had little success in putting his mind on his books.

On Monday morning David hurried off to school, having still not spoken about his troubles. Last night his father had not come home until late, and this morning David had not seen him while eating breakfast and before leaving the house. He was worried, because he knew he was in trouble and he knew his father should know about it. If charges were brought, his father would have to help David get a lawyer to defend himself.

Lonnie Webster was in David's physics class, which came in the first period. Lonnie said his mother was burned up with him.

"I tried to tell her," Lonnie said, "that being arrested as a juvenile doesn't mean anything. That's what the sergeant said. 'Course with you it's different, but we sure will back you up as witnesses and all."

David said he knew he could count on their being behind him. He only hoped they wouldn't be so far behind him that they wouldn't count. They laughed over that.

In the second period David had English. He felt so anxious to talk things over with Jimmy Hicks, and with anyone else who could give him information, that he cut his English class and went to the industrial arts wing of the building to look for him. He found Jimmy in the machine shop, where he was turning down the armature for a generator. Jimmy was good in auto mechanics. He worked at it part-time, and he always kept his mother's car in good shape.

"I don't know yet how much the repair job's gonna cost," he told David. "I went over to the place where they towed the car, and you know, every piece of glass on it is busted—windows, headlights, everything."

"Well, you know who did it," David said. "You ought to be able to make them pay for it."

Jimmy laughed, but there was no humor in his laughter.

"Make them pay?" he asked. "How do you make any white man pay for anything he does to one of us? If you don't get him while he's doing it—nail him right there, with witnesses—he can get away with anything. This is a white man's town."

David kept looking around, hoping to see the boy he had recognized as a Central High student at the drive-in. As he made his way through the crowded halls, he wondered if he would even be able to recognize the boy if he saw him. There were so many who looked like him—medium height, medium light-brown hair, medium weight, medium blue or brown eyes, he couldn't be sure which.

At noon he went to the cafeteria. He saw Maybelle there, but she was at a small table with three other girls. She smiled and waved at David, but it was obviously not the moment to talk to her. Neither Naomi nor Gertrude had come to school that day. He ate with Jimmy and Lonnie, and they were joined by others.

"Black man got no rights that a white man is bound to respect," one of them said. "Well, Davey boy, you did right. At least they know better now than to jump on somebody like you."

"Yes, but Jimmy's car is just about ruined," David said.

"We ought to make them guys pay for it," Lonnie said. "We know it was the same ones we had the fight with."

"Yes, we know, but how do you find them and then how do you prove it?"

"The guy at the gas station must have seen them. Maybe he even helped them."

"He said he didn't see anything." David was very bitter about it. "He said he didn't see anything, and he'll probably stick by that story right to the last."

"To the last?" Lonnie asked. "Maybe if he thinks that the last has come at last, maybe he'll change his story. Maybe if he figured that his glass and his pumps were going to be smashed if he didn't talk, maybe that would soften him up some."

"No!" Jimmy said quickly.

"We couldn't do anything like that," David said.

"I didn't say we ought to do it." Lonnie was smiling

broadly. "I only said suppose the guy thought we were going to smash up his place or even hurt him—just suppose."

David was not the first to tell his father about the trouble.

When he left school that afternoon at 3:10, his father was waiting in the car, parked across the street from the front door. David was walking with one of the girls who had been at the party, trying to give her a short rundown on what had happened. When he saw the car he knew that his father must have already heard the bad news. He said quickly to the girl, "See you later," and hurried across the street.

His father started talking without even pausing for a formal greeting. "Boy, why didn't you tell me?" he began. "Why you got to let the police department bring me the news, and let me look like a fool, not knowing what's going on?"

Sergeant Reed, he said, had telephoned asking that David get in touch with him at once. When Mr. Williams wanted to know what it was all about, Sergeant Reed had expressed surprise and then told him about the trouble on Saturday night. A complaint had been sworn out and signed, and David was going to have to appear in court to answer to a charge of battery.

David tried to explain that he just hadn't had a chance to talk to his father about what had happened.

His father started asking questions. David told him the story as they drove to police headquarters and parked the car in the limited-time zone. He told him what

Sergeant Reed had said, what the gas station attendant and the man at the Plantation had said and done; he even told him about Mrs. Hicks and her demands that David pay for the damages to the car.

When they went in the officer at the desk told them that Sergeant Reed was not in, but that he had left something for David Williams. He handed David the folded document marked "Complaint" without saying anything else. They did not examine the paper until they got back to the car.

The plaintiff was William Carpenter, age 28. He alleged that David Williams had assaulted him without cause, inflicting bodily damage, in violation of Section 483 of the Municipal Code. A hearing was set for April third, at 9:00 A.M. at the Municipal Court Building.

Mr. Williams said, "We'd better get a lawyer right away."

As the car moved south on Broad Street toward Mr. Taylor's law, real estate, and bail bond office, David sat beside his father, watching the slow-moving afternoon traffic. He remembered when he had been in trouble before. He supposed his father was also remembering that night, more than two years ago, when David had been arrested in a stolen car with John Henry Healey and an older boy known as Hap. Mr. Taylor had gone into juvenile court with the Williams family then. David's case had been dismissed. Healey had been sent to camp, and Hap—already on adult probation—had been sent to jail.

Actually David had been completely innocent. He had gotten into the car not knowing it was "hot." And in his present predicament he had no feeling of guilt. He could not agree with Sergeant Reed who had said he should have known better. He did not believe that going into a public eating place was at all like walking through a field of snakes. He believed that in court he would be found innocent. If, on the other hand, the court should find him guilty, it would only be because of race prejudice. A guilty verdict would convince him that Lonnie Webster was right: this was a white man's town.

They did not find Mr. Taylor in his office, but his secretary said he would call the Williams home later in the day.

When David had first come with his family to North Town, he had brought with him school records showing that he was a junior. However, the standards of his school and of the whole South were considered far behind those of Central High School. He had been put back a full year. Counselors had ignored his wish to prepare himself to go to college. He had been put into the general course, assigned to the classes that counselors thought a colored boy should have. It was not until he made good on the football team that he was considered as possible college material.

He sometimes wondered what would have happened had he been equipped with a smaller body and a bigger head. He could have been a real "brain," but he would still be taking vocational courses.

That Monday evening Lawyer Taylor did call Mr. Williams on the phone. An appointment was made.

After supper David was trying to study. He was working on physics. He wanted to get to his English assignment, which was a new book, a collection of stories and essays by colored writers. He knew he would enjoy that, but it was for reading when he had time.

Now at the kitchen table he was studying and making notes on the speed of light. It gave him a feeling of awe to recognize the degree of precision with which man can measure and plot results. He could barely understand what he was reading, and he knew that the facts of advanced physics were almost inconceivable to most people. Yet men were learning to understand the forces of nature, to select, control, and adjust them, and to measure and predict results.

He had the passing thought that in time—perhaps a not too distant time—it would be possible to understand man's behavior, to adjust it, and to forecast actions and results.

He heard someone at the front door. There was conversation, and then the heavy voice of Alonzo Webster came through. "That's all right, Mrs. Williams. We'll go right back."

Lonnie and Jimmy walked into the kitchen. He was glad to see them, but he knew that their visit would be the end of his study period.

"We've been talking, you know, about what we were saying today in school," Jimmy said. "Now Lonnie's got a good idea. I want you to hear it, man."

"This is the way I see it. Like Jimmy says, you and him have been talking already. So maybe what I've been thinking might make some sense."

David told him to go ahead.

"We don't really know who it was smashed up Jimmy's car," Lonnie said. "That is, we don't know the names of those people. Now I figure that that dude at the service station either he knows them or he don't know them. Right? If they're his friends, he can either tell us who they are or carry the message to them. Right? If he don't know them, if they're not his friends, then he's got no reason not to testify against them in court. Right?"

David nodded his agreement, although he wasn't sure what the next move should be.

Lonnie went on. "So Jimmy and I figured that it just wouldn't do any harm to go and talk to the dude."

David was fairly sure this wasn't a wise course to take, and he was shaking his head slowly in disagreement when Jimmy spoke up.

"Now, look," he said. "We wouldn't be planning any rough stuff. I know it would be silly to try to make him talk or even to threaten him. I wasn't thinking about that."

Together they discussed the possibilities. David explained that he knew the name of at least one of the men. He told them about the complaint.

"O.K. then." Lonnie and Jimmy both looked pleased. "That would make it easier still," Lonnie continued. "We could ask the man at the station if he knew the guy that was making the complaint. If they aren't friends, then we could persuade him to come on and do the right thing by Jimmy."

David said he did not believe the plan would work. Still, it might be worth a try. Maybe they could stop by there one night next week. At least, they could talk to the guy.

"No, we ought to do it now," Lonnie said excitedly. "Jimmy's got to get some money before he can get his car back."

David wanted to think over the idea some more. It wasn't clear to him that talking with a possible witness would necessarily help anything. He thought perhaps he ought to talk to Mr. Taylor and his own father first, before they went out to question someone who might well prove angry and hostile. So he told Lonnie and Jimmy he couldn't go. He didn't think it was too good an idea, anyway.

They argued, remembering to keep their voices low so that the others in the house would not hear. David did not want to be considered a coward. As a matter of fact, he said, there was little to be gained at best, and it could create a great deal of additional disturbance.

"Suppose they are friends, or even they aren't," he said. "This guy can go back to the whites and tell them anything he wants to. He can say we threatened him. He can go to the police. They're all white, and you know how it would be."

Jimmy didn't argue with him as much as Lonnie. All of Lonnie's talk centered around the point that Jimmy had to get some money to pay for the repairs on the car. David felt that he would rather dig down in his own pocket, or find some other way of paying, than go back and face the man at the service station who had already said he hadn't seen anything. When Lonnie suggested that David was afraid, David denied it but admitted it would take some real planning and perhaps some good advice before they should consider going out there again.

"I just can't help it," he said finally. "I can't see any point in our going out there and having any kind of talk or argument now. Maybe later, but not now. I won't do it."

Jimmy was disappointed; Lonnie was angry. Jimmy spoke of his mother's anger and her demands; Lonnie spoke of friendship and about letting people down. Then they pushed back their chairs and rose, ready to go.

Walking down the hall to the front door, they heard Mrs. Williams call, "It's raining again, boys. You're going to get wet." Both boys said they didn't mind.

Then Mr. Williams spoke up. "Well, David, maybe you'd better run them home in the car."

Lonnie and Jimmy thanked them warmly, saying again it wasn't necessary, but David put on his hat and coat and, without a word, led them out of the front door and around to the garage. Usually the car was parked in the driveway, but because no one had planned to use it tonight, Mr. Williams had put it away in the garage.

David knew where both boys lived. He planned to drop Lonnie off first and then go over to the other side of town to take Jimmy home.

It was Lonnie who said, "Why don't we go out by the service station and see if that dude is there?"

"What difference does it make?" David said. "I don't think it matters at all whether he's there tonight or not. We're not ready to talk with him, and I'm not going away out there to see him."

"Well, anyway," Lonnie insisted, "I'd like to see that service station again. I'd just like to be sure where it is. We won't stop if you don't want to."

If Jimmy had insisted, David would probably not have yielded. But Jimmy sat silent. He seemed to be unhappy. David decided he must be thinking about his mother's anger, her complaints, her demands that somebody pay for the car. He said, "Well, we might just drive by."

As soon as he had uttered the words he was sorry. He knew it would do no good, that it would only lead to further argument from Lonnie.

"I sure feel sorry for my boy Jimmy," Lonnie said. "Jimmy's momma can't afford to put up that money—two hundred dollars, maybe more. And then to think of some people who don't want to try to help Jimmy get somebody else to pay his honest debts. Looks like they trying to protect somebody."

As they drove out Broadway, rain was falling steadily. The brightly lighted service station was on their left. They looked at it as they went by, but they saw no movement at the gas pumps or in the glass-walled building.

Lonnie kept on talking. David tried not to listen to him. He was trying to "tune him out."

"Who are you trying to protect?" Lonnie asked. "Maybe you think you got to protect that white boy from me. I told you I wasn't going to do no more than speak to him."

David did not answer. At the next intersection he made a U-turn and started back. He was driving slowly, near the curb.

Lonnie spoke sharply. "You trying to protect that white boy?" he asked. Then he raised himself and put both hands on the steering wheel. "Whose side are you on, man?"

He was trying to take the control of the car from David, turning the wheel to the right so that it would go into the driveway. David could have fought back, but he knew it would create a disturbance out there at the edge of the street. He swung the car sharply to the right, lifting his foot off the gas, and coasted in, thinking that perhaps he would buy some gas. He was very unhappy.

Lonnie, who was in the middle, leaned over Jimmy Hicks, who was by the window. He opened the door and got out of the car. The service attendant, the same one who had been there on the night of their arrest, began walking toward the car. He was pulling a yellow slicker over his head.

Lonnie's voice boomed: "You remember me? You remember us three? We want to talk to you."

The man stopped, then took a step backward. He was near the cash drawer on the island where the two service pumps stood. He moved over toward the cash drawer and put a key in the lock. Moving quickly, he pulled out a gun.

"Yes, I remember you, you black niggers!"

Lonnie started back to the car. Jimmy swung the door wide; the car moved forward. As Lonnie's hand hit the side of the door, there was a bang that sounded like the crash of doom, louder than David imagined any gun could sound. He always remembered afterward how loud it sounded. Jimmy was dragging Lonnie into the car. The gun fired again, and as David stepped on the gas to get speed, he heard the gun behind repeatedly firing. Beside him Jimmy was saying over and over, "My God, my God, my God." Lonnie was groaning, not saying anything, just gasping and groaning.

Jimmy held on to Lonnie, saying over and over, "My

God, my God, my God."

Two blocks ahead, the light turned red. David did not slow up until he had almost reached the corner; then after looking both ways, he swung over to the left to get around. That was how he reached the driveway of General Hospital. He had never been at the emergency admissions door, but he had seen the sign, and it was to that door he drove.

A colored orderly came and helped them lift Lonnie out. Jimmy Hicks was smeared with blood. A pool of blood was on the floor. The orderly called for help, and they rolled Lonnie away on a wheeled stretcher.

Jimmy collapsed on a bench. He was crying, crying like a baby, but the only words that came from him were, "My God, my God, my God."

FOUR

ALONZO WEBSTER WAS DEAD.

David lived through a nightmare of policemen, reporters, lawyers, all wound together with anguish and regret.

For two nights and one day he was in jail.

The first night when his father came to see him David found himself unable to talk.

A guard had ordered him out of his cell in the basement; he led him along a corridor and up an iron stairway that rang like a tolled bell with each step. After a series of unlocking and relocking of doors, David found himself facing a barred and screened wall. Beyond the screen was an empty passageway, and on the other side of the passage and beyond another screen, David saw his father.

Mr. Williams had done all the talking. David said

nothing. He did not even try to see his father's face. He could not raise his head. He felt he was a disgrace to his family, doomed to a life of despair. He thought that it would have been better if he, rather than Lonnie, had been killed. Then all this sorrow would be over; all this grief would be done.

Later, when he was being taken back down the iron stairway, he remembered his father had said, "Your momma be praying for you."

David spent that first night alone in the basement cell. A strong odor of disinfectant hung in the warm air. A wash basin and a commode were attached firmly to the wall. Coarse denim-covered mattresses were on the four bunks. David thought he would be unable to sleep, that he would not want to lie on a mattress that might be germ-filled or alive with lice. He was tired. As he examined the beds, he decided that although the mattresses were stained, there were probably free from bugs. He stretched out on one of the lower bunks and slept.

He slept, and he dreamed.

Lonnie kept talking to him; Lonnie was laughing, teasing him and laughing at him. His voice was rasping; his laughter was part growl. Lonnie was talking to him, but his voice was far away, and as he laughed and danced around him, David kept trying to understand what Lonnie was saying. Lonnie's words were like pig Latin, but David knew Lonnie wanted to tell him something and that it was important. He wanted Lonnie to stop clowning. He tried to tell him. He wanted to say, "Make sense, man. Make sense"; and then Lonnie seemed to get the message, and he stopped laughing. He was still far away, but his face kept getting bigger and bigger like a movie close-up and Lonnie's head was going from side to side. His eyes were open wide, and David knew Lonnie was lost, and he tried to call to him, "Here! This way!" But now David realized he was very small, and although Lonnie's face was grotesque and of great size, he was still far away, and Lonnie was asking for help, and he was all mixed up. He wanted answers. Now David could catch some of the words. The words did not come from Lonnie's mouth, but David heard them and they were said in Lonnie's heavy bass voice.

"Whose side are you on?"

And David tried to answer, "I'm on your side, man." But he couldn't seem to raise his voice above a whisper and then he again heard Lonnie's voice, though Lonnie's mouth did not speak the words: "Whose town is this?" And David knew he should say, "It's our town!" and he struggled and twisted his body to get the words out, and he heard them come in a gasping choke from his throat: "Our town! Our town! Our town!" And then Lonnie's huge face filled David's whole view and became many faces of Lonnie, and all of them were twisted as though in pain and agony and fear, and they said altogether like the clanging of broken steel, "White man's town! White man's town! White man's town!"

And David could not make his voice heard, and he threw his body sideways and raised himself up on his elbows, gasping, "Our town, our town! It is our town. It's everybody's town."

He woke up, still half raised in the bunk. Then he remembered where he was, but he no longer felt that he was alone. He thought that Lonnie was in the room with him. He swung his feet to the floor and pulled himself up, peering into the empty spaces of the bunks above and across from him. His clothes were wet with perspiration. Swinging his arms, he took a few steps as though he were shadow-boxing and tried to clear his head.

The words he had heard seemed very real. The questions were Lonnie's. The answers were his, but on this hot night in a basement cell of the city jail, David Williams was far from sure that those answers were right.

At breakfast time the guard led him to the mess room. Other prisoners were there, all older than David, wearing blue denim pants and shirts—not all the same but giving the effect of uniform work clothes. Only David was dressed in street clothes. The others would know he was new, perhaps only temporarily held.

"What they got you for, man?" one of them asked.

There was silence while all the others seemed to be waiting for David to answer. They laughed when he said he did not know.

He stood in line and received a plate with beans, a chunk of bread, and a cup of coffee. He was surprised to find the coffee was hot and sweet, and the food edible. He was hungry.

There was little talk while the men ate; then quite suddenly all of them seemed to start talking at once, with boasting and defiance and bitter laughter shot through with obscenities. At the blowing of a whistle, they answered roll call and listened as a duty roster was announced. David's name was not called. He went back to his cell. The door was still open, and no one closed it after him.

He climbed into one of the upper bunks and lay on his back. He wanted to think. He searched for some understanding of what had happened, of what would happen, of what he could do to help himself.

He tried to remember what his father had said the night before. He could only recall—and that vaguely—the sight of his father beyond the two screens that separated them. He wished that by some miracle Lonnie Webster would turn out to be alive. Wasn't it possible that when they took him into the hospital he was just unconscious? Hadn't this sort of thing happened before?

Then he remembered the pool of blood on the floor of the car and the awful finality of the people at the hospital. Nobody had said, "He's badly hurt." They just said, "He's dead."

That morning Mr. Taylor came to see David. They sat on opposite sides of a long table. An officer was in the room, but he hardly glanced at them. David was glad to pour out the whole story and answer questions as the lawyer made notes on a yellow pad.

When the questions ceased, Mr. Taylor gave David his instructions.

"You are not to talk to anyone about your case," he said. "The police won't question you, but others might—reporters and men from the district attorney's office. It will be up to the D.A. to decide what charges will be filed and whether he will prosecute you. It is best for you to say nothing at this time. Tell them nothing.

"And don't tell the boys in the back, the other fellows locked up with you, anything about what happened, or later, even to your best friends outside. I'll talk to your folks, so they'll know."

David asked how long they would hold him.

"It's too soon to say," Mr. Taylor replied. "One person is dead. Nothing we can do now will change that. I'm sure you will be released, but I can't say when. I'm going to call in another lawyer. We need the kind of help that Jack Perlman can give. It may take some time to clear all this up. In the end I don't believe you will be held as criminally liable."

"Me? You mean me?" David rose to his seat to lean across the table toward Mr. Taylor. "How could I be guilty of anything?"

The lawyer motioned David back into his seat.

"I trust it won't come to that," he said. "We just have to know that under state law if a person is killed while in the act of committing a felony, his companions in the felony are sometimes held as liable as though they themselves had committed the killing."

"But Lonnie—Alonzo Webster—wasn't committing a felony. He was only trying to talk. He wasn't fighting, not even arguing. How can they say anything about a felony?"

"It could be said. It could be charged. Perhaps it cannot be proven. But we must be aware of every possibility."

David was led back to his cell, but not for long. Later

in the morning he was returned to the interview room. A well-dressed young man with a pleasant smile introduced himself as a deputy district attorney.

"I'm supposed to see you," the man said, "although there probably won't be anything new for you to say."

He offered a cigarette which David accepted—he felt that he needed it.

The man lit one for himself. He seemed to be very casual, almost friendly as he spoke.

"You know you don't have to talk to me," he said. "You have your constitutional rights. I guess we know the story pretty well. Still, if there's anything you want to explain about your part, I'll be glad to listen."

David said nothing.

"You, also, have the right to legal counsel," the man went on, watching David's face. "You can have a lawyer, and if you can't afford to pay for counsel, we'll see that you get one."

"Yes, I know." David sat up straight as he said it. "My folks got a lawyer for me. He was here this morning."

"So he advised you not to talk?" The district attorney's man was not smiling now.

"That's right."

"It's just as well." The man rose abruptly and walked toward the door. The guard let him out and then turned and led David back to his cell.

All the papers had the news on their front pages. The young man who had fired the shot that had killed Lonnie Webster and the other later shots, two of which had struck the car, was described as having been the victim of an attack by three Negroes. It was said that he had fired only in self-defense. The previous Saturday night's arrest and the case against David were skillfully built up. The man who had signed the complaint was quoted. He described the horrors of the attack at the Plantation Drive-In, where he had peacefully been sharing some late refreshments with a group of younger people. His account made it sound as if the three Negroes had charged in, demanding all sorts of special privileges, if not money. One would have had to read the article very carefully to realize that they were not robbers or holdup men.

This account was in the daily papers.

In the weekly paper published by and for Negroes were bold black headlines: "ANOTHER WHITE KILLER BLASTS NEGRO YOUTH."

By the time the afternoon meal was served, the other prisoners had no need to ask David why he was there. They had seen the papers, and they had heard the news reports. David was questioned; he was advised; he was offered cigarettes. When the meal was over, he was told he could go to the yard for recreation. He chose to return to the isolation of his cell.

It was the next morning, after a second miserable night in jail and after a second breakfast of beans, bread, and coffee, that David was released. He expected to find his father, and perhaps the lawyer, waiting for him. No one was there to meet him.

After they checked him out at the desk and gave him his property he thought of calling his family, but he decided to take the bus directly home instead.

He had never thought he would appreciate the fresh air of the city as much as he did that morning when he stepped outdoors. But he could not be happy. He was unsure of his status. Nothing had been said about bail. He had not been told when he should return or whether he should wait until called. As he stood on the corner of North Main Street, he remembered the words of his lawyer in the interview room: "We'll need the kind of help that Jack Perlman can give."

When he reached home, David found his mother frightened and worried. She greeted him with a cry of relief, and she held him close, feeling his arms and his shoulders. With eyes that were swollen and red, she gazed and gazed at him, at his face, his head, his hands.

He tried to reassure her. "I'm all right, Mom," he said, and in answer to her question, "No, they didn't hurt me."

He asked about his father.

"Didn't you see him?" Mrs. Williams asked. "He left early to go with Mr. Taylor to see another lawyer. He was with Mr. Taylor all day yesterday, too, trying to get you out. Wasn't he there? Or Mr. Taylor and the other lawyer?"

"I didn't see anyone I knew," David told her. "They just let me out; nobody told me anything."

They were standing in the hall. His mother was glad to have him at home, but they both knew that he was still in trouble. He asked about Alonzo Webster's family.

"Poor Mrs. Webster!" she turned her face away from her son. "I didn't know her before, but we went to see her last night. She's taking it right hard. They say the doctor had to give her some medicine."

Mrs. Williams started toward the kitchen. "You must be hungry," she said, "and you need a bath. Change your clothes, all of them, while I fix you something to eat."

David started up to his room. He was halfway up the stairs when he heard his mother speak again.

"David." She was leaning with one hand against the side of the door. Her other hand was raised to her face, half covering her mouth. "You know, Mrs. Webster wasn't herself. She didn't know who I was. She didn't get the name, and we didn't press it.

"She was going from one to another, asking the same question. She looked right at me and asked me why did it have to be her boy that the white folks killed. It hurt to see her so, but I was somehow glad she didn't know who I was."

In the late afternoon David called the Lenoir home, and Jeanette answered. He was eager to go see her at once, but she suggested that he come after dinner.

"My folks are just about as anxious to see you as I am," she told him.

David was uncertain about how he would be received. Mr. Lenoir, a post-office clerk who had transferred to North Town from New Orleans, had always been cordial to David as he was to all Jeanette's friends. David knew that Mr. Lenoir was ambitious for his children. Jeanette, the youngest of four, was the only child still living at home. Jeanette's two brothers had been graduated from college, and her married sister was living overseas with her husband, who was in the Air Force. Both Mr. and Mrs. Lenoir seemed to have every confidence in Jeanette; they trusted her; they believed she knew how to choose her friends.

Perhaps, David thought as he walked toward the Lenoir home at seven o'clock, perhaps this is the time when they will say Jeanette made a bad choice.

Mr. Lenoir was a thin man, light brown, with sharp features. He had deep-set eyes and heavy brows. Jeanette was like her father in that the lines of her face were angular, but she was like her mother in that she was dark in color, almost as dark as David.

When Jeanette led him into the living room, it looked as though Mr. and Mrs. Lenoir had been sitting there waiting for him, but as they greeted him, David felt the warmth of their friendship. They sat quietly and listened to him as he told them the details leading to the first arrest with Jeanette, then to the death of Alonzo and his own arrest and release. He answered their questions and he listened to what they had to say.

"I've talked to a lawyer about Jeanette's part in this," Mr. Lenoir said. "I did that on Sunday, and I talked with Mr. Taylor yesterday. I don't know if there'll be anything we can do, but I hope you'll let us know. There is a lot of tension. It's here, and I guess it's everywhere these days—North, South, in this country and around the world."

Mrs. Lenoir asked, "You don't think there will really be any big trouble here, do you? There wouldn't be a riot in North Town, would there?"

"You can't tell," Mr. Lenoir replied. "We have enough bad conditions, unemployment, and it gets worse instead of better—bad housing, more clashes, frustration, anger.

And then our young people have learned about democracy and freedom, and they want to have their part in it." He looked around with a smile as he said, "You see our David here, and our Jeanette, thought nothing of going out to the Plantation that night. They knew this was North Town, and they thought they had a perfect right to go there for hamburgers, just like anybody else. That started the cycle."

David said, "Jimmy Hick's mother says this is the white man's town."

"That's not so," Jeanette said quickly.

"Maybe that's part of the problem," Mr. Lenoir said. He wasn't smiling now. "Maybe there is a question about whose town it is, whose country, whose world, and some of us want to wrap it up and claim it exclusively for our own."

He asked David what he thought would happen next.

"My father and I have to see the lawyer tomorrow," David replied. "They'll bury Alonzo on Saturday. I went to see him at the funeral home today. I went to see his mother, too. She's taking it right hard I guess."

"Yes," Mrs. Lenoir said. "She's a mother. I don't remember Alonzo, although Jeanette tells me that he's been here. I guess I should make a call. What about the father? Is he here?"

"I've never seen him," David said. "He lives in Chicago." Then he added, "I guess they're divorced."

Mr. Lenoir rose. "Well, like I said, you and your folks keep in touch with us. I've seen some bad things myself, but we used to think they could only happen down South."

Before they left the room, Mr. Lenoir shook hands with

David, and Mrs. Lenoir walked over to him and kissed him. David stood silent for a moment after they had gone.

"They're great," he said to Jeanette. "Your folks. They treated me just like—" He had started to say "Like one of the family," but he stopped and finished with, "Just like I was another adult and their old friend."

"Yes, David Andrew Williams! So you're another adult and their old friend!" Jeanette teased him.

He tried at first to explain what he meant, but she seemed to understand, and since he was doing badly anyway, he gave up the attempt.

"Before all this happened, you were telling me that things had changed at school," Jeanette said. "What did you mean?"

"In a lot of ways, you can feel it," he said. "You know it's there, and you can feel it though it's mostly in little things.

"Take football: We had practice, and we had games, and on the field everything was O.K. Still, this year there was a difference in the locker room and when we were away on trips. Then in class and around the buildings, every time one of the big magazines—*Life,* or *Look,* or one of those—came out with a big spread on Negroes the white students kind of pulled away more.

"Then all the talk about ghettos and black power and about the riots! It seems like the whites look at a black and think right away that he's a rioter and that he's on relief.

"Sometimes I feel like standing up and spreading out my arms and hollering, 'Look, I'm American just like you are.' " David stood up and took the pose he described. " 'Look, I've got no bombs to throw, and I'm not on relief;

I work and my father works, and I'm going to school so I can make it in this land of the free; I don't want you to give me anything or take anything away from me; I'm a man and I'm an American.'

"That's what I'd like everyone to know, but more and more in school and on the street—yes, and in the magazines and on TV—white Americans are looking at black Americans as if they were some queer creatures just being discovered on the American scene."

"Seems like I've heard that speech before." Jeanette was smiling. "I have the strange feeling that this is where I came in. You used to talk like that when I first knew you. That was more than two years ago when you first came from the South."

"Yes I guess you're right." David sat down again. "I used to think I had to make a speech like that, and then after I got adjusted, I felt it wasn't necessary. That's what I mean about things tightening up. It's changing. It's as if they won't recognize that Negroes—or blacks, or whatever we're called—are people just like everyone else, that we're all Americans, and that while there are many disadvantages, some of us are making it."

"I know what you mean." Jeanette, who had spent her childhood in New Orleans, gone to high school in the North, and was now attending college, spoke seriously. "Still, they say you have to think about the majority. And when people talk about 'the Negro' they are trying to speak of something like the average. Maybe most blacks do have more disadvantages than you and I have."

"They say that those of us who have overcome some

of the handicaps should join with all the others in a mass movement. That's what the Reverend Moshombo says."

"I've heard about him—and about some of the others, too." Jeanette said. "We have a sociology professor who is very sharp. He has a Ph.D. from Harvard. He says that many speakers, many who sound very good while they're talking, are calling for united action, for unanimity. He says that unanimity is impossible in any society. He points out that it would be good if all of any people would agree on a program but that it's too much to hope for in the case of American blacks, some of whom grow up to be Republicans and some Democrats and some, I guess, even Communists. We're Baptist and Methodist and Catholic, too. Some of us are educated, and some almost entirely uneducated. We have a few millionaires, and we have a lot of people living in poverty. To get unanimity is impossible."

Five

On Saturday David missed a day of work at the hardware store. That was the day they buried Lonnie. When David called Sam Silverman to tell him he would not be in, Sam gave him a quick O.K. and said he would expect him the following week.

Lonnie had never been active in the Baptist Church, but his mother was a member, and at one time Lonnie had attended Sunday School.

At ten o'clock on Saturday morning, with the minister leading the way, David moved down the aisle sharing the weight of his friend's body in its gray cloth-covered box. He was the tallest of the six boys who had been asked to serve as pall bearers. His place was at the left back end of the coffin. After the casket was placed in front of the altar, the pall bearers were seated in the first pew on the left. Members of

Lonnie's family were on the right. The minister, the Reverend Hayes, was very solemn. He stood tall and straight at the rostrum as he intoned the opening words of scripture.

There were some hymns, a prayer or two, the reading of a short eulogy. It contained no reference to how Lonnie had died. It simply said, "He departed this life at North Town General Hospital."

David was not sure whether the Reverend Hayes then gave a sermon or simply an address. He read something from the Bible, and he talked about a mountain of cold hate in the land, a mountain that could be removed only by the warmth of love and understanding.

Ill will, suspicion, fear, uncontrolled anger, threats, and open acts of brutality that called for other acts of brutality, he said, would never allow peace to come to the children of God. He did not say that people must learn to turn the other cheek, but this was the idea that David got. He did not use the term nonviolent, but he did suggest that there was a better way than fighting back.

David listened. He felt guilty. He believed he had been weak in yielding to Lonnie's desire to go back to the service station. He knew that he had wanted to go and also that he had been afraid. Now he realized that there had really been something to be afraid of. He wished Lonnie had been a little more afraid and not so insistent, yet he felt this was being disloyal to his friend. What they had done might even have been right.

The scent of flowers hung heavy in the air. It was not like the scent of flowers in a garden. In some strange way these flowers had the smell of death.

The organ was playing softly when they came out, walking up the aisle with the body of Alonzo, the minister ahead, intoning the words of the Twenty-third Psalm.

"The Lord is my shepherd; I shall not want."

Mrs. Webster was sobbing softly as she walked behind the casket with Lonnie's father, who had come from Chicago for the funeral.

"He maketh me to lie down in green pastures; he leadeth me beside the still waters."

David saw the church filled with people. There were many men as well as women.

"He restoreth my soul; he leadeth me in the paths of righteousness for his name's sake."

Many men, young and old, had come to the funeral. Their faces were stern.

"Yea, though I walk through the valley of the shadow of death, I will fear no evil; for thou art with me; thy rod and thy staff, they comfort me."

They were near the back of the church. David heard murmured comments from those standing in the pews: "That's what the whites do to our people."

"Thou preparest a table before me in the presence of mine enemies: thou anointest my head with oil; my cup runneth over."

In the lobby: "How long we got to take it?"

"Surely goodness and mercy shall follow me all the days of my life: and I shall dwell in the house of the Lord forever."

At the hearse, as David was lifting the body of his friend, he heard someone behind him say, "This is a white man's town."

While something deep inside him wanted to say, "No!

No! No!" David heard again the echo of Lonnie's angry voice saying, "Whose side are you on, man?"

On Monday, the first day back at school after his arrest, David presented his written excuse to his homeroom teacher. Mrs. Wynkoop read it. She handed it back to him and told him he would have to go to the office to see the attendance clerk. No one in the room said anything about being glad to see him. Some of his classmates looked at him with no change of expression whatever. Most of them were busy doing something else.

"Well, I guess that's the way it will be for a while," he told himself as his long legs carried him down the hall toward the office.

When he got his chance to speak to the attendance clerk, she told him, without looking at the note, that the principal, Mr. Hart, wanted to see him. He was shown into the office where Mr. Hart was seated at his desk as though he had been waiting for him.

"Well, David Williams," he said, without asking David to have a seat or offering any word of greeting. "We were not sure you would be back. In fact, we are not sure we can take you back. Don't you have some charges standing against you?"

Mr. Hart had always been friendly to David, and his words were something of a shock.

"Why, I guess so," David answered with hesitation. "I know there's going to be a hearing, but that will be on the third of April. I didn't want to miss all my school work up to that time. Besides, Mr. Hart, I'm innocent."

"Yes, Williams." Mr. Hart seemed overly severe. "That's what they always say, always the denials, always the 'I didn't do it.' I hear that kind of talk from you people all the time."

"But it's true, Mr. Hart." David was hurt by the principal's attitude. "It's true, and I'm going to prove it. I have my witnesses."

"Yes, no doubt, you have. Some of your friends who were with you, I suppose." As David started to answer, Mr. Hart slapped his hand down on the desk. "Never mind. I'm not going to hear any argument from you. And I'm not going to have a trial here. The judge will handle that in due time."

David wondered why he had been summoned to the office, but Mr. Hart soon explained that. He hesitated for just a moment, and then he went on.

"I'm not going to keep you out of school at this time. I could do it. You are already eighteen years of age. We don't have to keep you here. You know that, don't you?"

David's eyes were filling with tears. His voice was weak and did not carry the assurance he wished it might as he said, "But I haven't done anything wrong, Mr. Hart."

"Yes, that's what they all say." Mr. Hart spoke in a harsh voice. "And I'm not prejudiced, either. I'm as fair as a man can be. Just the same, I will not tolerate violence and misconduct on the part of you people or any other people. You're going to have your chance in court. We're going to let you stay in school for the present, but you may not be graduated. We'll be watching you. Anything out of line either here or out in the community will mean the end of your stay at Central. This goes for you, and for any of your friends who get mixed up in attacking law-abiding citizens for any reason. Now I hope you understand that."

David swallowed hard. Mr. Hart's unfairness cut deep. He said, "I understand," and left.

In the school cafeteria the two tables at the north end were usually used by colored students. There was no rule about colored students eating at special tables. Some of them ate with white friends, but most of them sat together at these two tables, each of which seated eight persons. White students never ate at these tables, and most of the colored students never ate anywhere else.

David often lunched with his colored classmates, but he was also frequently invited to eat with his friends among the white students, who welcomed him especially after he made the football team. Today when he went into the cafeteria, no white student smiled or indicated by a nod or a word that he would be welcome at any of their tables. Even the colored students when he sat down at one of their tables did not greet him with any show of pleasure.

Jimmy Hicks was not there. Jimmy was a leader among the group at the table. He had always been outspoken in expressing his dislike for white people. He often argued with David about his friendliness with the "paddies."

Those at the table wanted to learn the latest news.

"Jimmy told me yesterday," Gertrude Smith said, "that he's not coming back to school. He says he has to try to get a job to help his mother with the young ones."

"It's just like Lonnie used to say," one of the boys volunteered. "The white man thinks he owns the town, and everything in it. He can do what he wants with us, even kill us whenever he gets mad, and we're not supposed to do anything in return."

"They sure got Lonnie," Gertrude said.

"But one day, maybe soon, the colored people here are going to get wise and start fighting back, taking what belongs to them," the same boy said.

"Fighting back?" David asked. "That's how all this got built up, some people think. You know Jimmy's mother says I shouldn't have fought back when they jumped me out there at the Plantation ten days ago. She says that's why her car got smashed up and Lonnie is now dead and all of us are in trouble. Sometimes I think she's right."

"She ain't the first little bit right," another of the boys said. "Only trouble is, we got to fight back together. When we fight back individually, they can take us, but not if we fight back together like we ought."

"That's what I say," a third boy added. "When anything like that happens we ought all to get together and maybe take a dozen cars out to a place like the Plantation and wreck the damn thing. You know, make a Watts out of it. That's what we have to do. Look what they do in other cities, New York and Detroit and lots more."

"Yeah, black power can sure show strength when we get together," Naomi spoke up. "Look what they say about it in *Life* magazine. They say that's the way the Negro gains his dignity. Some of them say it's the first time they really felt they were standing up like men."

"They sure took over in Newark, too!"

David remembered the magazine articles. He remembered that some of those who had been quoted had talked of the sense of dignity they had achieved. He also remembered that other Negroes had spoken of the businesses that had been destroyed, the jobs lost, and the awful statistics—thousands arrested, thousands more wounded and hospitalized, and people killed by the tens and twenties and thirties and forties. Most of those killed were Negroes. He had thought as he read the stories that this was a high price to pay. He had wondered then if there was not another way. He had thought about Martin Luther King and nonviolence. He had hear Mrs. Hicks say, "Turn and give them your backside."

David wasn't a coward. He felt that if anyone could take a stand and prove anything he could too. He listened now to the discussion around him. They were lively words, brave words, but they did not make much sense. He wished Lonnie were here. As he stared across the table at a vacant chair, he knew he would never forget Lonnie's questions: "Who are you trying to protect? . . . Whose side are you on?"

In the days that followed, David was aware of people looking at him in a new way.

He was used to having people look at him, even stare at him sometimes when they did not know him. It had bothered him when he first came from the South, where he had never gone to school with any but colored people. He was self-conscious, and he felt awkward. Tall and dark, he was noticeable in any crowd. He supposed that people looked at him, wondering what he was going to do or say next. It seemed sometimes as if they wanted him to go into an act, perhaps a song and dance or else suddenly be bad, striking out and throwing things.

He remembered that when he first came to Central he had been surprised to find that the white students were not so different from the colored boys and girls he had known down at Pocahontas County Training School in South Town. Down South he had thought that the white students would be extra smart. He had thought that he might not be able to keep up with them in classwork. By the end of the first semester he had realized that while some of the white students were "brains," some of them were very dull and unable to make passing grades. Most of them were just about average. In some of his classes David managed to excel. He studied hard and was able to do well.

In his second year David made the football team. He was not great, but he was good in his position at end. It had not been easy. On his first attempt he had completely failed. Still, he had finally made it. Then it had been necessary for him to work hard to hold his place. People in school had become friendly. They had stared less, and they had smiled and greeted him more often.

Now they had changed again.

Some who had been friendly turned away at his approach. Some he had scarcely known at all looked at him with something like suspicion—perhaps even hate. At his approach some of the girls moved away as though they were afraid of him.

Becky Goldberg was not like the others. She had asked Maybelle Reed about David the first day the story was in the newspapers.

"I don't know anything about it," Maybelle replied.

"Not any more than I read in the papers."

"But all three of the boys were at your house just before the whole thing started."

"Oh, that!" Maybelle tossed her head and fluttered her eyelashes. "Lots of kids were at my house that night. It didn't have anything to do with the fight."

Everybody at Central knew that Becky was a girl with a mind of her own. It was a good mind; Becky had a reputation as a "brain." Assistant editor of the paper, captain of the debating team, and member of the senate, Becky campaigned for student rights, labor rights, and civil rights, all of which she spoke of as human rights. She was opposed to the draft, and she editorialized against required attendance at religious observances. She also took the part of Mary, the mother of Jesus, in the Christmas pageant.

She had few close friends, but everybody, students and faculty alike, respected her. David was among those who admired Becky.

"She's all right," he once said to his mother. "At the rally she played the guitar, and we sang spirituals, and, you know, that gal knew the words better than I did. She's all right."

Becky called to David one afternoon just as he was turning to go into the physics lab. She walked in with him and climbed on a stool beside him, announcing that she had to get the whole story from him.

"Not for the paper, I hope." David said with a show of alarm.

"Not for the paper," Becky agreed. "I'm not being a reporter. I'm just a concerned human being. I need to know."

As David talked, Becky kept interrupting to ask questions. She wanted details. Several times she nodded and said, "I knew it wasn't like the papers said. I knew it couldn't be." The period was half over when she turned away to go to her own class.

"You'll come out all right," she said. "And don't let old Hart-less worry you. You'll be right in line for your diploma with the rest, come the great day."

On his third day back at school David's homeroom teacher told him that Coach Henderson wanted to see him when classes were over at 3:10.

David had a warm feeling for the coach. He was a hard man, and at one time he had seemed to be overhasty in judgment. But David had learned that Coach Henderson wanted to be fair. He had told David he didn't care at all what color a man's skin was, so long as he could play football. Well, this was not the football season, and David was sure that it wasn't about football that Henderson wanted to talk today. He was glad the coach had asked to see him.

As he crossed the gymnasium toward the phys. ed. office, Henderson was talking to some basketball players. He waved in greeting. David went on to the office door, where he stood until the coach was free. He had only a short time to wait. Henderson motioned him inside and closed the door.

"Sit down, Williams," he started. "Take the load off your feet. So I hear there's been some trouble. You want to talk about it?"

"I don't know just what to say, Coach Henderson,"

David replied. "I guess there's a lot I could say, but then"—he shrugged his shoulders—"what's the good of more talk?"

"I guess I know what you mean." Henderson sounded as though he understood. "I'm not a lawyer, of course, and I don't know if there is anything I can do. I've been thinking, though. Generally we never hear the other side of the story. I'm just not ready to believe that what the papers have said is the whole truth. Would you like to tell me yourself what happened?"

David figured he had nothing to lose. His lawyers had advised him not to talk, but the coach was willing to act as a friend. The principal had asked him nothing; Mr. Hart had just told him. Remembering how twisted the newspaper accounts had been, David decided he would give the coach an account of what had happened.

He did not repeat everything that had been said, but he described the way he had been pushed and shoved in the hamburger place, how they had been arrested, and in more detail, how he had gone back to the service station.

"And I can swear," he concluded, "I can swear on my life, though nobody may believe it, that only Lonnie got out of the car and that neither he nor any of the rest of us had anything like a weapon. I guess the man was scared, maybe—though he didn't have any real cause to be. He had the gun, and he just started shooting. And that's the God's truth. I swear it."

"So," the coach said and sat thinking. "So that's how it was. Williams, I believe you. I believe you because I know what kind of a guy you are. When you see fellows working out on the team and playing in football games, you can tell what they're like. You can tell. You're not a liar, and you're not a coward. I know that, and I believe you."

"Then if you believe me, Coach, you must know that the papers and the radio have lied. That's what it's been—just lies. And here at the school it looks as if everybody just automatically believes what he reads. Nobody else on the faculty has even asked me what happened. It seems as if in their eyes they believe that I'm guilty of everything the newspapers said. It seems as if they hate me. I don't understand it."

The coach said that he could understand how people reading the newspapers and hearing the news on radio and television would accept what was reported. He could almost understand why the reporters told a one-sided story.

"You know, I've been seeing unfairness and the reactions of prejudice for a long time. And if I don't say anything around here, it isn't because I don't know about it. Now I can understand to some extent how you feel. I don't claim to understand how colored people keep themselves under control. I expect that most of us would be fighting mad all the time. I expect the way things are it's just normal for colored people to be angry. I can't say that I blame them. There must be an answer though, a way to go, something like negotiation and reason."

"Dr. King preached nonviolence for a long time," David replied. "And he died knowing that reasoning doesn't overcome racism. No, sir. It takes something more than talk."

"I wonder if you're right, Williams. Many people have

been moved; many have given up their prejudices—their racism if you want to call it that. Perhaps you have more friends than you know. Perhaps the Negro has more friends than he can count."

David remembered something, from another time, another place. Down South white people had come to stand with him and his family when they had been in trouble. A white man had died in the conflict. Another white man had said, "It ain't every white man that's against colored folks."

"But, Coach Henderson, there's so many of the other kind. And it looks like the other kind are riding high, wide, and handsome. It looks like they want to insist this is a white man's world. I thought I had made some real friends here at school. But now that I'm in trouble, none of my teachers, not even the principal, nobody but you, has even asked me to tell them what happened."

"But, Williams, you have to realize that none of the other teachers, nobody on the faculty, knows you as well as I do."

"Do they have to know me so well? Why should they believe everything bad about me until they know me well? Can white people only trust Negroes they know well? Most white people don't try to get acquainted. In fact, they try right hard not to know colored people. If what you say is true, things look bad. It looks like things are going to get worse. It looks like there will be more breakdowns. It looks like maybe more riots are going to break out."

"I don't want to hear that kind of talk, Williams." Henderson was very serious now. He got to his feet and walked across the room and turned back. "Not from you. For God's sake, not from you. Don't let yourself get sucked into any of that, not even that kind of talk. Keep away from people who are talking about fighting back and riots breaking out. I can understand how they feel. But not you, Williams, not you."

David had been ready to talk, really to talk man to man with Coach Henderson. Now he found it impossible. There was a chasm between them or a wall, a high stone wall. The coach's words rang sharp; they hit him like blows in the face: "Not you"; "That kind of talk"; "Keep away." David felt that the coach was another white man who wanted him to be nothing but a "good nigger," a "happy darkey," smiling, shuffling, satisfied.

He tried to explain, but Henderson would no longer listen.

"Don't you understand that I'm black, too?" David asked, and he tried to explain that he was one of the millions of victims of race prejudice and hate, but the coach did not hear him.

He wanted to say, to shout it out loud, "This is my country as much as it is yours. Why can't you understand?"

The coach outtalked him, and David again heard, "not from you" and "keep away from them" and "don't be bitter."

He talked a little more, but he didn't really say anything. When he left, he could hear the heavy voice of Lonnie asking questions.

Back on the job at the hardware store that next Saturday David tried to do his work well. He moved a little faster than usual. No one asked him any questions about his troubles.

He thought the other clerks and the bookkeeper were watching him, and he felt they were not as friendly. Before his arrest they had made joking remarks about his height. David could reach things far higher on the shelves than anyone else. They had made some cracks about how great he and John Bowman would be working together. Well, David had shared in the jokes, knowing that he was well over six feet and knowing that he was not as strong as the vigorous John Bowman, who was a powerful two-hundred-pounder.

Even John Bowman made no attempt to talk to David until late in the day. At lunchtime he said nothing about going out to get soul food. David went down the street and ate two cheeseburgers; on the way back to the store he bought a two-quart container of milk from which he drank during the afternoon. Just before closing time, John moved over to work beside him.

"I got to talk to you, boy," he said.

With a nervous laugh David said, "Well, O.K. Talk then."

"Not here, man. After we close up. I'll see you outside."

At six o'clock John seemed to have forgotten what he had said. He was one of the first to leave, slipping out before Sam locked the door. He left with a smile and a joke. David helped with some putting away and cleaning up. He and Sam went out at the same time. Sam, turning to be sure that the door was secure, called a cheery good night over his shoulder, and David walked down toward the bus stop. He was wondering where John Bowman was.

As he waited for the bus, a car pulled up. Big John

Bowman was at the wheel. Two other men were in the front seat with him. One of them opened the rear door, and John called to David. David had seen both of the men before. He knew they were friends of John's. One of them worked where David's father worked, at the Foundation Iron and Machine plant.

"Couldn't talk to you in the store," John Bowman said. "I want to talk to you, and my friends do, too. In fact, there's lots of us want to know what the hell happened."

David said the lawyers had advised him against making any statements, but he guessed it was all right to talk to his friends.

"Yeah, them lawyers, they all work together. They got the town locked up," Green, the man who worked at Foundation, said. "You got to depend on some real friends, some brothers."

The other man said, "And we mean by brothers, blood brothers."

"That's it man." Bowman turned to look at David. "That's it. We're going to take you on home now. You don't have to say anything to your folks about it. We're coming back later though. We're going to have a meeting at eight o'clock tonight. I'll pick you up in time to go."

David said he supposed that would be all right.

"You know the last time I asked you to go to a meeting was the night you got into trouble," Bowman reminded him." If you had been with us, you wouldn't be in all this mess right now."

David said he supposed that was so but you never could tell.

He was afraid that he might have trouble explaining to his father about the kind of meeting he was going to attend. But no explanation was needed: Mr. Williams was not at home for dinner that evening; he had gone to a union meeting. The Foundation plant had not called the laid-off people back to work. The union was holding a lot of meetings, but there was little they could do.

A little before eight o'clock John Bowman, with David sitting beside him, was driving uptown. He turned east to go straight out Sixth Street, beyond the house where the Williams family had lived, through a small business section and out beyond to an area where there were many large privately owned houses. The car had almost reached the city limits when John braked quickly, slowed, and turned off the pavement into a driveway beside a large frame house. He turned off the lights as he drove toward the rear. It was only after the car reached the back of the house that David saw several other cars there.

"This is it," John said. "Looks like there's a lot of people here already."

David had asked earlier what kind of meeting it was, and John had answered, "Just a meeting of some of the brothers."

They walked up the steps to the back porch.

"Brother Jack?" John said as he moved toward the door.

"That you, Brother Bowman?" David saw that a man, a lookout perhaps, was seated in the dark.

"That's right," Bowman answered, "and I brought a new member."

David did not challenge the statement. He was sure that he was not a new member of anything. He was certainly not a new member of a brotherhood that met secretly in the dark of night and had to have guards or sentries at the door. He wished he had not come, but he could not run away.

John led the way through a dimly lighted hall and then opened a door into a crowded room where the air was thick with smoke and heavy with loud talk. One of the men David had seen earlier, Green, came toward them saying he was glad David had made it. Others turned and looked, waving at Bowman and staring at David. It was as though they had been expecting him. Their looks were neither friendly nor hostile—rather, they were curious. Bowman was telling David that he was really going to see something now, that these were true brothers, that he could rest easy because he was among friends.

As if on signal the room became quiet. The eyes of all turned toward the door that led to the front of the house. It opened. Into the room came a tall figure wearing a white robe with the emblem of a raised clenched fist. It was the Reverend Moshombo, whom David had heard at the Community Center. There was a ripple of applause. Behind the robed figure came the same two powerful men who had been with him on the platform at the Center. This time they were not wearing robes. They were dressed in dark suits, with white shirts and conservative ties; they looked as if they might be business or professional men—ministers, perhaps teachers, or doctors.

Green, who had been talking with John, moved forward to greet Moshombo. The two men shook hands and talked together. When Green lifted his hands in the air and asked everyone to be seated, it reminded David of a small church service.

Green then announced that they had come together tonight to meet with their leader, the Reverend Moshombo, and to consider "what the black man is facing and what solutions we can find to our problems to avoid extermination from the face of the earth." He said that tonight they were also going to hear the real story of the latest assault of the white man on black brothers, an assault which had already resulted in the death of one fine youth, one who would have been "a warrior in the battle for freedom and a soldier in the cause of defense."

First, however, he called for reports. The finance committee reported that a final check of the meeting two weeks earlier showed a balance of eleven hundred dollars. There was applause.

The membership chairman reported a gain of 220 members since the last meeting. He said that many others were interested in joining, but because of the lay-off at the Foundation Iron and Machine Works, people were short of funds.

Someone suggested that a special exemption be made for the benefit of those who were laid off from their jobs. Another argued that those who were laid off should not be granted any more privileges than those who had not been working at all. He said, "I haven't had a job for over a year, and nobody offered me any exemption."

Finally the Reverend Moshombo was presented. Everyone stood as he raised his hand in a clenched-fist salute. Most of those present raised their hands in answer.

David did not. He noticed that Big John Bowman did and that he shouted a hearty hail as well.

Moshombo began to speak. He spoke slowly and with intense feeling. His words came so softly that they would not have been heard if those in the room had not listened carefully. He talked briefly about the oppressions which "all of us have borne," and he wound up with the prophecy that "Ethiopia shall rise again." To bring this to pass, he said quietly, it would be necessary for the black man to be united in the brotherhood, as the fingers of the hand are united in the center of the hand, from which the fingers spring. Formed together in a mass, they could gain full freedom.

Moshombo, looking toward David, spoke of "our heroic freedom fighter." The men applauded.

Then Green rose to say, "We now come to the place of listening to a report on the slaying of one of our youth." In concluding the introduction of David, he said, "Our own David Williams even now stands in jeopardy of the hangman's noose held over his head by the white man's law. We must never let that noose tighten around this brother's neck. No, never! We will pledge our lives to his defense."

There were cheers and applause as David found himself moving forward toward the table.

He was afraid. He had been in danger before, but never had he admitted that he was afraid. Now he knew he was frightened. These men who called themselves brothers seemed to be demanding something from him and threatening him with harm if he failed to give them what they wanted.

His opening remarks were awkward. He stumbled

over his words, but after a few moments he steadied and fell into a sort of story-telling form, recounting what had taken place, first at the hamburger place and then at the service station. He did not attempt to make a speech; he just told them what had happened.

The Reverend Moshombo questioned him.

"Did you boys have any weapons at all?" "Any guns?" "Any knives?" David answered they had not.

Moshombo then asked about the police. Whether there had been any brutality? How about when they were searched? Had the police searched the girls?

David knew that the girls had been searched at the police headquarters by a woman. He answered that they had been searched. He did not explain when or how.

The questions and answers affected the crowd. They spoke out in anger and bitterness. David would like to have said something more reasonable and he would like to have asked that they not make up their minds until the trial. But he knew that there was nothing that he could say to quiet these men who had gathered together so that they might bitterly denounce everything connected with the white man. He knew his father would not have come here, and he knew that Mr. Williams would be very angry if he found that David had been at this meeting. David wondered if perhaps his father was what they called an Uncle Tom.

No, he could be sure that his father was not a coward. He had been through a great deal, and he had stood up like a man, refusing to crawl, refusing to take low even when he faced sure and swift attack.

And yet his father was less hostile and angry than John Bowman. David knew there was a difference. His father would have his own answers to Lonnie's questions "Who is it you're trying to protect?" "Whose town is this?" He wasn't sure how his father would have answered, and he thought he would probably disagree with him, but he knew his father would be very sure of himself. That was the way he was.

When the meeting was over the true brothers crowded around David, shaking his hand, promising support. "We are all with you in this thing," they kept saying.

But how they were going to be with him in his troubles, in his trial, no one said.

THE BIG LAYOFF AT FOUNDATION had taken place at the end of the second week in February. More than four thousand workers had been let go then. That was half the work force at the plant; it was also a large percentage of North Town's working population. To have so many workers sent home and told not to return until further notice meant hardship throughout the town. The state unemployment insurance offices put on extra help to meet the sudden rush of applications. They operated with a high degree of efficiency, and the unemployment checks came out regularly. For most of the workers, however, their unemployment payments were less than half of their usual paychecks, so while they could still eat and remain in the houses they occupied, they could not pay all of their bills. Those who were buying houses and had large monthly mortgage payments to meet were hardest hit. They had to plead for time. Landlords, bankers, finance companies, and other holders of notes moved to guard their investments. The Welfare Department protected families from eviction for nonpayment of rent; the relief program was supposed to see that no one went hungry. Just the same, people felt the pinch, and some said they were facing disaster.

The members of the Williams family had considered themselves fortunate in being able to meet their bills and to have the two children in school and Mrs. Williams at home rather than at work.

Now David's trouble meant more expense. Both the lawyers had to be paid a fee, which they called a retainer. Neither of them would discuss what the final cost would be. Mr. Taylor, who knew the family very well, assured Mr. Williams that Mr. Perlman would be reasonable.

In March a few of the old employees at the plant were called back to work. But Mr. Williams was not among them. He continued to draw his weekly unemployment insurance checks. He did not like it.

"Makes you feel like you're getting relief," he said. "You have to stand in line and answer questions about how much you made or didn't make. All the men try to act like it don't matter. They laugh, but it ain't funny, I tell you." He longed to find some sort of work to do, even if he earned no more than the unemployment check covered.

At first he spent his spare time at home, doing some of the things he had always planned to do but hadn't yet gotten around to. He painted the front hall and stairway.

He put more shelves in some of the closets. He cleaned out the basement and made shelves and racks on which to hang up tools. In the afternoon and evening he went out and visited some of his friends. Sometimes he did not come home for dinner, and his family knew that he had accepted an invitation to eat at someone else's house. Sometimes when he returned, he smelled of alcohol. He was not a drinking man. At the Baptist Church where he was active in the Men's Club, they said he would be made a deacon. No one could say now that he was a drinking man, but he had always enjoyed a glass of beer and sometimes now he drank hard liquor with his friends. He boasted that he knew how much to take, and he never came home loud or looking as if he were drunk.

When he had his friends over, they would sit talking, sometimes drinking beer and playing cards.

One evening David's mother suggested that she should go to work.

"No," Mr. Williams said. "We don't have to do that. Besides, I don't want my wife going to work in some white folks' kitchen."

He said it, and he meant it.

"It's not like it would be permanent," Mrs. Williams said. "Just until you get called back."

"If a man is a man he ought to be able to take care of his family," Mr. Williams said. "I've been working steady on a regular job. Looks like I will be soon again. It's not right for my wife to have to go out and take care of somebody else's family. We got our own kids."

David agreed. He wanted his mother to stay at home

in her own kitchen, which she seemed to love so much. He offered to drop out of school, but his father pointed out there were no jobs. For David to leave school would do no good.

"Besides," Mr. Williams said, "you the one who has got to get us out of this mess. You the one who's got to get good schooling, so when we get old we can look on you as our protector and our everlasting provider."

David laughed at the way his father put it. As a matter of fact, they all knew that he had often said that parents shouldn't depend on their children and they knew, too, that he expected to be able to provide for himself and his wife without having to depend on his son. But they also knew that he was ambitious for David and eager to see him get his high school diploma, go on to college and then to medical school. It was partly with this idea in mind that they had left the South.

David wanted to go on to college and medical school, too. And he also wanted his mother to be able to stay at home and not have to go out to work.

But Mrs. Williams made her own decision. She knew how to clean and how to iron. It wasn't hard for her to get work. She went to Stanton Park where she got housework to do by the day in a number of homes.

Ed Williams was unhappy. He stayed away from home more and more. He stayed out later at night. He was sullen and difficult. On Sundays he did not want to go to church. He sometimes said that his head hurt or that he was tired. No one ever asked him what he was tired from—but he did not go to church.

Other men were being called back to work.

Next door lived a white family name Bernadette. Mr. Bernadette had worked at the Foundation plant for many years; he was near retirement age. His children were all grown and only he and his wife now lived at home. Mr. Bernadette had laughed when he was laid off, saying that he needed a winter vacation anyway. He was among those called back first.

"Seniority," Mr. Williams said. "He's got seniority. Been at it a long time, so he gets called back first."

David remembered having heard, "Last to be hired, first to be fired." Now he heard people say, "Last called back will be the man that is black."

At first Mr. Williams complained to his friends about his wife going to work. But most of his friends disagreed.

"That's what a wife is suppose to do," Mrs. Crutchfield said. "A wife is suppose to help out. That is, if she's worth her salt. And I know there ain't a lazy bone in Fannie Williams's body."

Mrs. Crutchfield did not go out to work. She was much older than David's mother. She and her husband had left South Town many years ago.

Mr. Crutchfield was a trusted employee at Foundation, a lead man in the maintenance crew. "They can't get along without me," he said with a laugh. "I am what you call essential. I go off on my vacation, and when I come back, the place looks like it's falling down."

David knew what Andy Crutchfield meant. David had worked at the plant under his supervision. He was a hard-driving man. He himself worked hard, and he demanded good work from his crew. David could understand why Mr. Crutchfield felt himself essential and why he worked that way.

At first Mrs. Williams went to work with a friend from church. David would drive her down to the corner of Broadway and Main where she met Mrs. Walker, and together they would take the bus to Stanton Park. Then his mother said that was too much trouble. She insisted on walking to get the bus on Washington Street and then transferring on Broadway. She returned the same way. After a few days she seemed to know her way quite well, and she said she could get along all right.

Sometimes when she came home, she would be very tired. Betty Jane and David did more and more of the housework. Their father prodded them. He no longer did any work himself, but he saw to it that they did. That is, he did at first. After a while he seemed to notice less and less, and spoke very little. It was plain that he was worried.

Betty Jane and David were preparing a dinner of canned baked beans and frankfurters one evening when their mother came home, looking especially tired. She only murmured a greeting and went directly to her room. Their father was still out, probably at the union hall or with some of his friends. A place was set at the table for him. David was trying to be cheerful, for Betty Jane, but his jokes did not sound funny even to him.

Betty Jane went to the stairway to call her mother. Soon Mrs. Williams came down, saying that she had a headache.

As she sat at the table, she did not talk. Betty Jane looked hurt. David felt worried and anxious.

He tried to make conversation. "Where did you work today, Ma?"

"Oh, at the Barclays'," she answered.

Betty Jane clapped her hands. "That's the beautiful house that sits way back in the yard, isn't it? The one you had us go look at from the outside last Sunday?"

"Yes." Mrs. Williams's voice was flat. "Yes, that's the one. I won't be going back there anymore, I guess."

"What's the matter?" Betty Jane asked. "I thought Mrs. Barclay and the folks there were so nice."

"Maybe they're not so nice. Maybe they're like the others." She would say no more about what had happened.

After Betty Jane had gone to bed, Mrs. Williams called David from the dining room where he was studying, into the kitchen were she was ironing.

"You ought to know, David," she said, "it looks like white people are pretty upset about the way things are going. Mrs. Barclay said today that us colored people are pushing too fast. She told me she'd let me know when she wanted me again."

"Yes, I know," David said, nodding his head. "And maybe she does think we're pushing too fast. But I don't think we've been pushing fast enough or hard enough."

"She says that she is all for fair play and everybody having his rights, but she believes things have gotten, as she says, out of hand. I didn't try to argue with her." Mrs. Williams shook her head. "You know how white people are—especially women."

She went on to say that Mr. Barclay was a lawyer and that Mrs. Barclay seemed to be pretty smart, too. She had been talking about the terrible way the young people were acting. Then when she started to talk about the crimes of Negroes, she became excited.

"She and I, just the two of us, were there," Mrs. Williams said. "I was cleaning silver in the kitchen. But she was talking real loud, and she said, " 'Mr. Barclay told me about three colored men the other night who attacked a man in a service station and one of them got killed.' And she said, 'It served him right.' "

David could see tears in his mother's eyes. She was trembling as she picked up a dampened shirt and shook it out. She spread the shirt on the board and started ironing again, before she went on:

"Well, I had to tell her. I told her it just wasn't so. And I guess I told her back just about as loud as she was talking to me. And she said how do I know so much about it like her husband." Mrs. Williams looked up. There were tears welling from her eyes and rolling down her cheeks, but David saw that she was smiling. "I told her my own boy, my own son, was one of the boys that was there, and I told her how it was."

She went on with her ironing. She folded the shirt over. David still said nothing. He knew his mother was not through telling the story.

"I said, 'I'm Fannie Williams, and David Williams is my boy.' And I told her that my boy is as honest as the day is long. And that it is the white folks believing anything and everything about colored people that makes it so hard. And I told her we were all tired of the way our people were treated. And I told her that was the reason we moved away from down South. And I told her the white folks in the North were about the same as they were in the South, not willing to recognize that black people can be honest and honorable, too. And I guess I told her a lot of other things besides, but I couldn't help it, and I'm glad I told her."

David was glad, too. They talked for a while, and when he left his mother to go up to bed, she kissed him good night. He said, "Ma, I'm proud of you."

They did not tell David's father about the incident in the Barclay home. They knew it would make him angry. He already felt shamed that he was not providing adequately for his family; he would insist that his wife give up her work.

But Mrs. Williams knew that her earnings were important. She was buying groceries and paying bills—and Easter was coming. She wanted her family to have some new clothes for that festive day.

Easter came early that year. The winter had not been cold, but there was a lot of snow. David had made some extra money shoveling snow from sidewalks. His father had gotten some days of work with the city in the snow-removal crew. The pay was that of a laborer—and Ed Williams had been used to earning a machinist's pay. But he shrugged off the difference.

"Every little bit helps, as the old lady said," he remarked.

After the snow came heavy rain. With the rain came strong winds, and it was cold. In the house they had to remember to close doors, so they could keep the heat down to save on fuel.

To David the days did not seem like the approach of Easter. He remembered Easter down South.

In the rural South Easter had marked a season of spring rejoicing. The weather would be mild. Pasture lands would be green, and fruit trees would be in blossom. People would be plowing for the planting of cash crops, cotton, and tobacco, and for the garden crops that grew close to the house. Using their credit, they would buy seeds, fertilizers, equipment, and sometimes lumber for the repair of their houses and barns. Charges would be entered on the books against the sale of the crops. There was one other important item to purchase, the new clothes. It seemed that everybody had to have new clothes.

Those who could afford to pay cash studied the Sears Roebuck and Montgomery Ward mail-order catalogs. They made their selection and sent them off with post office money orders and waited eagerly for the big packages. In David's family they always ordered early, hoping the choices would be satisfactory and the sizes correct. Mr. Williams teased his wife because it seemed she never got the right size, color, and style on the first try. Something always had to go back, and this took time.

Betty Jane had everything new for Easter. She would get at least one new dress, often a coat, certainly a hat, and a pair of Sunday shoes. Then there would be a supply of undergarments and hosiery. David would have a new suit, some shirts, sometimes an overcoat or a topcoat, and usually a stout pair of shoes.

Mrs. Williams always got something new. She seldom felt she should buy a whole new outfit. But she would dress in her best on Easter, and only the members of her family or her closest friends would be able to tell which part of her outfit was not brand-new.

Everyone knew that Easter was a religious festival, and almost everyone went to church. People went to church on Easter who would not be seen there again until the following Easter—unless there happened to be a funeral or wedding in the family.

Everyone knew Easter was a religious celebration, but few were in a truly religious frame of mind. They seemed rather to be filled with the spirit of spring and with the hope that the new plantings would be more successful than they had ever been before, that this year's additional debt would be wiped out by bumper crops, that the budding new life and the warm sunshine would calm the aching pains in the joints of the aged, bring young hearts together, and make men more kindly disposed toward their brothers.

Easter was a time to be happy. That's how David remembered it. In the house they spoke of Easters "at home," meaning when they lived on the little patch of ground that now seemed so precious to them.

While Mrs. Williams worked with the hope of making Easter bright for her family, David was thinking of a few extra days of work—and it was in the Easter vacation that he was to be tried on charges of battery at the Plantation Drive-In.

Then he received a notice to attend the coroner's inquest on the death of Alonzo Webster. It was to be held at nine in the morning on the third day of April, the same day and hour that David was to appear in municipal court. The conflict in time and date disturbed both David and Mr. Williams, but Mr. Taylor assured them it would be worked out. They were to meet downtown at Mr. Perlman's office at eight-thirty on Monday morning.

On Sunday afternoon David went to see Jimmy Hicks. Jimmy had also received a notice, but he did not have a lawyer.

"God knows I can't afford no lawyer for Jimmy now," Mrs. Hicks said. She was sitting at the table in the kitchen, drinking coffee. "If he got to go around acting like a fool, he just have to take what comes."

Neither David nor Jimmy tried to argue with her.

"That first time it wasn't my Jimmy's fault," she insisted. "It wasn't him that started no fight. It was the fighting that caused all the mess. And he didn't start no fight. Now on account of you starting a fight I got no car, and the finance company is claiming I got to pay for it anyhow."

She said she was going to stand right behind her Jimmy as far as the car went and that she was sure looking for David Williams to come up with the money to pay for it.

"But this other thing," she said, "he taken that on hisself. I got no money for no lawyer, and if they want to send him away, they just have to send him. I can't do nothing about it."

David said that his family had already engaged a lawyer—two lawyers, in fact.

"You will come with Jimmy tomorrow, won't you, Mrs. Hicks?" David asked.

"No, I ain't going to no courthouse." Mrs. Hicks got

up from the table and walked over to the stove and poured herself another cup of coffee. "I ain't going to nobody's courthouse. I don't never go to a courthouse if I can help it. I know what they do to you down there. Besides, I got to work. I got to go to work with all my bills and all my troubles. I can't be laying off to go hanging around no courthouse."

Early Monday morning Jimmy went with David and Mr. Williams to Lawyer Perlman's office.

Mr. Perlman was busy in the back, but he came out to greet them, saying he would see them in a little while. When Mr. Taylor arrived, he went directly into the rear office. A few minutes later he and Mr. Perlman came out.

"Mr. Perlman has to be in superior court this morning," Mr. Taylor said, "but he will go into municipal court to represent you in the battery complaint. I'll be with you at the inquest on Alonzo Webster's death."

Mr. Perlman wished them luck as they left.

The inquest was to be held in the basement of the county courthouse. The hall leading toward the room was poorly lighted; the passageway was narrow, crowded with filing cabinets and packing cases. A photographer walking backward snapped pictures of Mr. Taylor leading the way, and of David and Jimmy and Mr. Williams. David thought of throwing his hands or his forearm over his face, but he knew he had nothing to hide. He tried very hard to look confident. But he did not feel confident.

As they entered the crowded hearing room, Mr. Taylor

spoke to a bailiff who had four persons, one of whom was John Bowman, move from the second row at the left to make room for these important people. John Bowman spoke to David and he smiled, but they had no conversation. The service station attendant was seated in the first row on the right-hand side of the aisle. He was dressed in a clean blue suit with a white shirt and a dark tie. David could not see his face directly, but as the man turned to speak to an older man beside him, David noted that he must be very young.

All the seats in the small room were taken. People were standing at the back of the ten rows of chairs, and around the sides of the room. David saw John Bowman raise his hand in a suggestion of a clenched fist. He was smiling as he made the gesture. It was not a thing that anyone else would have noticed. One of the men with him was a leader in the brotherhood. David saw others whom he knew; one of them was Head.

At the long table across the front of the room two clerks were already seated. They were looking at some papers piled before them. In the center of the table another neat pile of papers was awaiting the coroner who would preside at the hearing. They had not long to wait.

A door opened behind the table and a small man with tight features entered, leading five men and three women, who made up the coroner's jury. They took seats on the raised platform at the right of the room.

One of the clerks at the table stood and read a document that stated that this hearing had been assembled to examine evidence and to determine the cause of death of

Alonzo Webster on or about the twenty-seventh day of February; that all persons having knowledge of the cause of death and/or the circumstances of death should now present that evidence; that withholding knowledge or giving false information constituted a crime in violation of the written and the common law of the state and that those who gave false testimony could be held for perjury.

The clerk announced that as witnesses were called they were to step forward to be put under oath. The coroner, presiding at the table, would question them.

The first witness was Lonnie's mother, who testified that the body she had seen at General Hospital was that of her son, Alonzo Webster. A man from the medical examiner's office then read the autopsy report that had been received and entered in the record. The bullet that had caused Lonnie's death was displayed. It, too, was entered as evidence.

An inspector of police was called, and he fixed the time and place of the shooting as reported to him by Craig Davenport, male, white, age 23, and by David Andrew Williams, male, Negro, age 18, and by James Hicks, male, Negro, age 17.

The coroner then called Craig Davenport, the man who had fired the gun. As he rose, an older man beside him also rose, introducing himself as William E. Barclay, attorney for the witness. At this point Mr. Taylor stood and introduced himself as attorney for the witnesses Williams and Hicks.

The two lawyers exchanged courteous nods. The coroner, however, seemed disturbed.

"I hope you gentlemen understand," he said, "that we are not conducting a trial here. We're just trying to get information about how this Webster boy happened to get killed. A representative of the district attorney's office is here, but only as an observer. If there's any prosecution, that's his job later. This hearing is only to get information."

Both lawyers agreed that they understood the circumstances. Mr. Barclay said that all were anxious to get at the truth of the matter. He promised full cooperation. He offered to question the witness in order to avoid irrelevant and immaterial testimony.

"Counsel is aware, I am sure," the coroner said, "that the coroner questions the witnesses. However, if there are no objections from opposing counsel, I believe we might proceed with such a plan, the usual rules of evidence being recognized and observed."

When Mr. Davenport was seated in the witness chair, Mr. Barclay started his questioning: name, date of birth, occupation, and so on. Then he asked Davenport where he was on the night of February twenty-seventh, a Monday. He asked if he had seen on that night a person later identified as Alonzo Webster. He asked if Alonzo Webster had approached him. He also asked if he had seen David Andrew Williams and James Hicks. Having received affirmative answers to all of these questions, he next asked if Davenport had been placed in a position of danger by these three persons. The affirmative response was hardly audible.

The lawyer turned to face the coroner. "Now, young man," he said to Davenport, "we know that these details are very unpleasant, but it is necessary to establish just what happened that night. And for the sake of accuracy in the record we will have to ask that you speak clearly and loudly enough for all to hear."

Then he asked Davenport to explain how the he was placed in danger.

"They were coming at me," Davenport said.

Mr. Taylor was on his feet. "I object. May I ask that the witness not use the plural pronoun *they,* but specify by name, and further that he clarify the statement, 'They were coming at me.' "

Mr. Barclay nodded in pleasant agreement and asked that Mr. Davenport make his statement more specific.

But Davenport seemed to be afraid. He was clearly very nervous. His voice was husky as it came from his throat. He said, "I mean they, all three of them, were running at me, and I told them to get back and they kept on coming."

"Now, now," Mr. Barclay said. "You don't have to tell the whole thing just now, Mr. Davenport. We just want to establish who was moving toward you."

"Well, it was that one, Webster, I guess." Davenport paused, and then he pointed. "And those two there. I don't know which one is Williams and which one is the other one, but it was the three of them."

"And did they say anything?" asked Mr. Barclay.

"Yes, they said something but I'm not sure. It was all about 'we're going to get you,' and things like that."

"We're going to get you?" Mr. Barclay repeated.

"Yes, and like that."

"So when they said they were going to get you, did

you have any idea what they were talking about?"

By the time Mr. Barclay asked the question, Mr. Taylor was on his feet saying, "I object. We are dealing with the facts of a shooting and a death. We do not want speculation about ideas."

Mr. Barclay bowed in agreement and offered to withdraw the question.

"Now, had you ever seen these three persons before?" he asked.

When he had received an affirmative answer, he pursued this line with further questions as to when and under what circumstances.

Davenport described the Saturday night event, saying that at 1:00 A.M. the police had chased a car into the station; that these same three persons had been arrested along with three colored girls; that they had left their car on the premises; that sometime later that same night they had returned with a police officer and at that time the car had been found to be damaged. He said he had told them he did not know who had damaged the car.

Mr. Barclay asked Davenport to describe details of the shooting, and although Mr. Taylor raised objections, Davenport did get into the record that he believed his life was in danger. He also said that he had given a warning: "Get back or I'll shoot."

Mr. Barclay said he was through with the witness. Then Mr. Taylor asked the coroner if he might question Davenport further. Mr. Barclay objected. He called attention to the fact that this was not a trial and there could be no denial that a Negro had been shot and that this witness had fired the pistol that killed him. He said there was little more to add to that. Mr. Taylor insisted that it was necessary to question the witness, and the coroner, looking uncomfortable and worried, said he supposed that it was counsel's right to question.

Mr. Taylor started asking Davenport almost the same questions that his own lawyer had asked him. He started each of his questions, "Now did I understand you to say. . . ."

Davenport answered in the affirmative. He kept looking at Mr. Barclay as though seeking advice. There was little for Mr. Barclay to object to because the questions were only a repetition of Davenport's earlier testimony.

Then Mr. Taylor got to the Monday night of the shooting.

"Did I understand you to say that the three young men, that is, Webster, Williams and Hicks, were coming at you?" he asked.

Davenport dropped his head. Then he turned toward Barclay and said, "Yes, they were coming at me."

"Now can you tell us whether they were all coming from the front toward you?"

"Yes, all three were coming at me."

"All from the front toward you?"

"Yes, yes, all from the front. All three were coming at me."

"Were they three in a line, one behind the other, maybe Indian file? Or were they three abreast in a line?"

"It was kind of in a line, kind of bunched up, all of them coming at me together."

"And where were you as they were coming at you?"

"It was kind of over that way," Davenport said with a gesture.

"We have to get this down on the record, Mr. Davenport," Mr. Taylor explained as though to a child. "We have to say it was toward the street or it was away from the street or toward the island where the pumps are. Can you say it in words so it can be entered in the record?"

Davenport seemed to be very relieved now as he specified that the car was toward the curb and it was about one car length inside the curve of the driveway.

Mr. Taylor listened very carefully, and then he said, "Mr. Davenport, this is very important. If you were near the island, you must have seen the car as it drove in from the street. Is that correct?"

Davenport answered with a nod.

"Now when the car door opened on the passenger side how many people did you see get out?"

"One, that was the fellow Webster."

"And did you see anyone get out on the driver's side?"

"No. I didn't see anybody get out on that side."

"Then if only one got out on the right side and nobody got out on the left side, how can you say that three men were moving toward you?"

"I object. I object." Mr. Barclay was on his feet. "Counsel is trying to confuse the witness and avoid the truth of the situation."

Mr. Taylor only shook his head slowly as he watched Davenport who was obviously confused and very unhappy. When the objections of Barclay were not accepted by the coroner, Mr. Taylor went on:

"Now, young man, I'm sure you realize that you are under oath, and I'm sure you want to tell the truth. You understand you are not on trial. We know it is altogether possible that you were frightened and surprised and you felt that you were in danger on that fatal Monday night, but it is important also that we know the truth about the other people who were present. I refer to David Andrew Williams and James Hicks. It is important that we know the truth about where they were. Now, can you say that you saw these two young persons, as well as Alonzo Webster, moving toward you before you fired the gun?"

"Well it looked like they were. It looked like they were. And I didn't know what they were going to do. Everybody was hollering. And it looked like they were coming at me."

There were no further questions, and Davenport was excused. He was trembling. He looked as though he needed the help of the bailiff, who took his arm and led him back to his seat.

Mr. Taylor called for the witness James Hicks. He asked enough questions to establish that James Hicks was the driver of the car that was in the service station on the prior Saturday night, that it was damaged by breakage of practically all visible glass, that the cost of the repairs was $208, and that on Saturday night the witness Davenport had been in attendance at the service station, but that he had reported he did not know who had damaged the car. Then Mr. Taylor went on to the events of Monday.

"Mr. Hicks, will you tell us why you and your companions went to the service station at 8:25 P.M. on February twenty-seventh?"

"Well, it was like this," Jimmy said. "We figured that

this man at the service station must have known who it was that smashed up the car, and Lonnie thought we should talk to him about it. Lonnie said we just ought to go out there and talk to him. Lonnie just wanted to find out more from him, so maybe we could collect something from the people who had done the damage."

Mr. Taylor asked two further questions. He asked who got out of the car, and he asked if either James Hicks or David Williams had left the car.

"When Mr. Taylor was through with Jimmy as a witness, Mr. Barclay questioned him. He wanted to know just where Lonnie had been sitting in the car.

"Lonnie was sitting in the middle—like between me and David Williams."

"Then how did Webster get out of the car without you stepping down first?"

"When the car stopped," Jimmy said, "Lonnie just crossed over and climbed out over me. He got out, but I didn't put my foot on the ground, and neither did David."

David was the last witness. He answered Mr. Taylor's questions in very much the same way as Jimmy had.

When Mr. Barclay started questioning David, it was clear that this lawyer was questioning the truth of the claim that they had gone there because Lonnie wanted to talk. Mr. Barclay wanted to know just what Lonnie had said. He tried to confuse David, but David remembered it all very clearly. Mr. Barclay asked when Lonnie had first made the suggestion that they go to the service station and talk, and David told about the visit to his home, and the fact that it was raining and that this was why his parents suggested that he drive the boys home. David did not want to make Lonnie look bad, so he did not emphasize his own reluctance. More and more, David had come to realize that he had been very fearful that night. Though he had certainly never thought that anyone would be killed, or that anyone would use a gun, he had thought that any confrontation would only result in more trouble. That is what he had wanted to avoid.

While Mr. Barclay questioned David, Mr. Taylor made no objections. David answered the questions, saying, "I'm not sure about his exact words," but he did repeat what had been said.

Mr. Barclay seemed to suggest that David was evading his questions by saying that he could not remember the exact words. Still he continued to interrogate him.

"You seem to be an intelligent person," he said finally. "You remember all the details. According to your statements, it seems as if you should be able to remember exactly something that Alonzo Webster said, something he said to you directly. Now I want you to tell us just what you do remember he said with his own mouth."

David dropped his head. He did remember something. He remembered, and it hurt. He remembered a question that Lonnie had asked, and it was a question that he himself could not at this point answer. He did not want to repeat it. He raised his head and looked around. Those seated in the audience were staring. They were looking at a show, and he was a performer. At the back of the room his friends were waiting like spectators at a game, pulling emotionally for their own side. From the middle of the room a familiar face caught his eye. Wearing dark glasses and a hat that made her look older, Becky Goldberg leaned forward in her seat. Her head was thrown back, and her chin was high. She was not smiling.

David's voice was taut, but the words came clear.

"Just before we turned into the station, Alonzo might have been mad at me because I hadn't wanted to go along, and he asked me, 'Whose side are you on? ' "

There were no other witnesses. The hearing was adjourned while the jury retired to deliberate. Most of the people went out.

As David and Jimmy Hicks with Mr. Taylor and Mr. Williams left the room, John Bowman joined them outside the door. He introduced his companions, and they agreed that David had done well on the witness stand.

" 'Course, you got nothing to worry about," John Bowman said, "but that white boy, he ought to be sent up for life. That wasn't nothing but murder. You know they not going to do anything to him, though. They'll just say a white man killed another black man, and that will be all there is to it."

David knew he did have something to worry about. He did not try to explain to John Bowman that he and James Hicks would be in jeopardy if the story of the three of them joining in an assault was believed.

In less than thirty minutes the bailiff called all parties back to their places. The jury filed in. The coroner called for the verdict, and one man stood and read from a paper. "We the jury find that Alonzo Webster died as the result of gunshot fired by Craig Davenport; we further find that the action of Craig Davenport was justifiable homicide."

Someone in the back of the room said, "No!"

The coroner struck the table with his gavel. The bailiff moved toward the back of the room and ordered those present to be quiet.

David's father leaned over and put his hand on David's knee, and the lawyer said, "It was to be expected. It was to be expected."

SEVEN

LAWYER PERLMAN NEVER TOLD the Williams family how he had handled the battery complaint in municipal court. His secretary simply called the house to say that the case had been dismissed. The news loosened some of their tensions.

They still feared, though, that serious charges could be filed as a result of Alonzo Webster's death. "We must be aware of every possibility," Mr. Taylor had said early in the case.

After the hearing he talked with David and his father.

"I don't believe the D.A. is going to file on the basis of death sustained during the commission of a felony," he said. "He probably knows that he couldn't sustain a felony charge."

"Then that means it's all over?" David asked.

"No, I'm sorry." The lawyer shook his head. "The D.A. will hold the action in abeyance. If the press or the police department should put pressure on him, he might file later. Also if either you or the Hicks boy were to get involved in another arrest, this case might be activated."

"It ain't right," Mr. Williams said. "It's a threat. The case ought to be dismissed. It's like something hanging over the boy's head—just because he's colored."

"Yes," Mr. Taylor agreed. "We can hope, though, that there will be no further trouble."

In spite of his troubles, his worries, and his absences, David had not neglected his schoolwork. It had been hard, with extra hours of studying at night and more attention to the papers he turned in. His conduct had been as near perfect as he could make it.

There was nothing to block his graduation, and he believed there could be nothing to stand between him and a scholarship at State College. The scholarship called for a generous work-aid plan as well as help for athletes. In January, Mr. Hart, as well as coach Henderson, had promised endorsement. Unless the principal had changed his mind, David felt he had nothing to worry about.

At the office when David went to see Mr. Hart, his secretary said the principal was busy. It was a week before he was able to get an appointment.

"I have a report on you, Williams," Mr. Hart said. "You seem to be maintaining a satisfactory level in classwork and conduct. If you keep this up, you will be allowed to stay in school, at least until the end of the semester."

This wasn't enough. David's face showed his

disappointment. It may have shown anger, too. Mr. Hart spoke sharply. "We haven't decided yet about your graduation."

"I thought you said it would depend on the court, Mr. Hart. I wasn't guilty. The case was dismissed. That was on the third of April."

"A technical matter. We know there are tricks that lawyers use to get their clients freed. What was done in court has no bearing upon your character, but our diplomas do certify worthiness, and the faculty committee doesn't give them out without due consideration. I don't promise that you will have a diploma. Better not count on it."

"But Mr. Hart"—David felt the words choking in his throat. "I've got to go to college. You said . . . about a scholarship . . . you would help."

"That was before you showed your true self. We never suspected you were to join the criminals who attack decent citizens. Well, I'll tell you, Williams, you people have declared war on my country, and I'm not willing to increase your strength if you're going to use it to overcome me." Mr. Hart rose from his chair.

"I am not prejudiced, but I am the principal of Central High School, North Town, and I am not going to recommend anybody for anything unless he has proved himself worthy," he said.

There was nothing more to be said. David would have liked to have been able to question Mr. Hart and make a statement. He would have liked to ask, "How do you prove?" "Who else in the graduating class has had to prove his worth?" "How many obstacles must we overcome? How many bars must we clear? How many hurdles are ahead?"

Perhaps it was useless to ask such questions. Perhaps it was useless to try to explain.

He thought about it as he sat later that day in history class with Miss Madigan. He liked Miss Madigan. She was one teacher who encouraged discussion, and she seemed to be impartial and impersonal.

"Now, of course, you will understand," she said when they were discussing the riots, "you will understand that here we don't have anything like the conditions in other places. Some cities have regular ghettos, where the slum conditions are very bad. The unemployment situation among Negroes in the ghettos is always bad, and then they had some very radical Negroes."

David sat looking straight ahead, trying hard not to act as though he knew what race violence was and that he himself had lived in the ghetto in North Town, that some of those seated in this very class were still living in the ghetto. He could not forget that many of those living there were now unemployed and that some had been out of work so long that they had lost hope of finding regular jobs and establishing a regular work program.

For a minute or two no one spoke. One boy, Joe Redman, slumped deep in his seat and chewed gum as though his mind were far away. David knew that Joe was listening, that he was taking everything in, that he was going to be talking about it later, and that Joe was even now thinking of epithets and curses that he would like to bring down upon Miss Madigan's graying head.

"My father says"—Marie Shultz was speaking—"he says that in Watts, in California, it's just like down South. He says that most of the Negroes are right off the plantations, and they don't know anything about living in the city or working in factories and stores."

"Well, you must realize," Miss Madigan answered, "that most of the Negroes from the South like to live in a warm climate. That's why they go to California. Now, you see, we don't have many real Southern Negroes here."

David felt that he had to speak. He looked hard at Miss Madigan and tried to catch her eye. She saw him but went right on talking, "Of course, there are exceptions." She turned to David as she spoke. "There are always exceptions to the rule, but on the whole, I think that the Negroes in North Town are doing very well and that they don't have too many complaints."

David knew that on the east side most of the people were living in poverty. There were an awful lot of men who were unemployed. He knew that even at the Foundation plant most Negroes were employed at unskilled jobs and that they had special problems in being upgraded or promoted. Even his father, who was an excellent machinist, had still received only a second-class machinist's pay. The plant hired janitors and cleanup men who were paid at the rate of common laborers.

He supposed that colored people in North Town did live better than those in Watts and perhaps better than those in Detroit. Perhaps that was why the people in those cities had rioted. But he wondered at the wisdom of such action. He had read of the number of people killed, and he knew that most of those who had died were black people. He knew, too, that the areas damaged by fire were where Negroes lived, that stores and factories had been burned out. It seemed that the problems were only intensified by a riot. He wished he knew more about it.

He did not know at that time that his own city would be torn by strife. Later, after the North Town riot, he wondered about that day in class. He wondered what would have happened if he had risen in his seat and said to Miss Madigan and all those present, "You just don't know. You just don't know. Conditions here are as bad as they were in Watts, and right here the sky will be blown off before too long."

He didn't say it—he never had the chance to say it—but he wondered later what would have happened if he had.

David knew that he was in trouble at North Central, but he had learned that you shouldn't stop. It was one of the things Coach Henderson had drilled into the members of the football team: "You don't stop. You don't ever stop."

It was like a slogan. It was like a banner to the team. That spring it became for David something to hold on to: "You don't stop. You don't ever stop."

He was not giving up. He knew he would not stop. But he did want the chance to talk over things. He wanted to talk to his father.

That was not easy. It used to be easy, but since his father's layoff, and increasingly as he found himself waiting, hoping but losing some of his hope each day, Mr. Williams was becoming bitter. He stayed away from home more and more, smoking heavily and drinking, too.

He seldom talked with David or Betty Jane. He never joked with them. He no longer teased his wife or gave her compliments about her cooking.

He had boasted, even in the South, that he was a man able to provide for his wife and his children. He was the head of the family, the breadwinner, the leader and protector.

He saw his wife going to work now almost every day in the homes of white people. He saw her return in the evening, exhausted, trying to keep up with the tasks in her own home as well as those at work. The money she earned was important. It amounted to more than the weekly unemployment insurance that Mr. Williams drew.

David's mother knew that some of the good feeling in the family was slipping away. She had no time to prepare good things for the table, and the family rarely assembled to eat a meal together. About the only time the family ate a meal together without rushing was at breakfast on Sunday. Mrs. Williams tried, and usually was successful, in making that a happy time for all of them. She was glad to see that when her husband and her man-sized son were being well fed, they would talk freely. Still, they did not sound optimistic about conditions.

"Maybe we'd better think about moving," Mr. Williams said while he waited for his second serving of waffles and sausage. "They say Foundation is tooling up with a lot of new machines—automated ones. You just get them set, and they run themselves, and one man with these machines can turn out more than five men, or maybe even ten, the way we used to work."

"But you're a good machinist," Betty Jane said.

"Everybody knows you can run the machines as well as anybody, probably better."

"Maybe so, but it's the seniority. It's the old hands—the ones who've been there ten years, some of them twenty—they're the ones getting the training now. They won't need to call all of us back."

"So that means"—David looked across at his father—"that means the ones without a lot of seniority—really most of the colored men—might not get back on."

"That's what it comes to." Then his father was quick to add, "But it's got nothing to do with race. I would have seniority, too, if I had come up North a long time ago."

Mrs. Williams said, "If we move now, you'll have to start all over again. Maybe they'll be calling you back soon anyway. Besides, with David graduating, and maybe getting a scholarship for State College, we couldn't very well pull up stakes now.

"But I'm not doing a man's part—not working, depending on unemployment money, same as relief, and on my wife's earnings, and maybe my son's. I don't like you wearing yourself out over other people's wants," Mr. Williams said.

"Oh, it's not so bad." Mrs. Williams wanted to make her husband feel better. "It's not so bad. I'm beginning to get used to it."

"Well, I don't want you to get used to it," Mr. Williams said loudly as he shoved himself back from the table. "Maybe I'm getting used to it, too. Maybe we all are. I see men like that, used to their women working, and they're no damn good—no good for themselves or for anybody else. In this house we're not about to get too used to it. I hope, never."

He rose from the table to leave the room.

Betty Jane called to him. They heard him stamping up the stairs; then the door of the bedroom slammed. When he came down again, he was buttoning a clean shirt, getting ready to go out. He walked around as he talked. No one answered him.

"I see them around the streets, doing nothing, going no place, sometimes on relief, mostly depending on their wives. I see them. They stand on the street, in the bars and the poolrooms, and then drinking when they do have the money, 'cause what else is there for them to do? They say 'I don't care,' 'I don't give a damn,' but you know what? They're caring all right; they're crying inside. They're sick in their hearts, and they're scared, too. Scared that it won't be any better next week or next month or next year. Scared that their kids won't have anything to live for and no jobs to go to. I say they're scared; never mind about, 'I don't care.' They're just whistling in the dark. They're laughing to keep from crying. They're scared and their hope is gone."

He had reached the back door, car keys in hand. He turned to say, "Well, I tell you, I don't want to get used to it."

EIGHT

IN JUNE DAVID WAS GRADUATED.

The coming and passing of graduation day was less thrilling than David had thought it would be. For so long it had seemed to be far away, especially after the threat that he might not receive a diploma. On the last day of final examinations, when he saw his name on the list, his relief was enormous. At school only Becky Goldberg said anything to him about it. With a wave of the hand and a pleasant smile, she said, "I told you."

The great day came swiftly. Gowning. Rehearsals. Marching with music. Speeches. The long walk across the platform. The audience in the crowded auditorium had been asked not to applaud until all the class had received their diplomas, but when David's name was called and he started toward Mr. Hart, he heard clapping out front. It was only a short burst of sound, perhaps from his parents who were unable to restrain themselves.

The Reeds had asked David to Maybelle's graduation party. The invitations they sent out were very formal, with "R.S.V.P." engraved in the lower left-hand corner.

At school David spoke to Maybelle in the hall. "I got the invitation," he said, "and thanks very much, but I think I won't be able to make it. I may be going out of town with my folks."

"Oh, gee! I'm sorry." Maybelle tossed her curls and flashed her teeth. "I'm real sorry. I thought you would bring Jeanette. But by then"—her head went on one side as though she were thinking out loud—"by then Buck Taylor will be back. I guess he could bring Jeanette."

David knew that he wasn't going out of town, and he knew that Maybelle was not sorry that he would not be at her party. He would have liked to be with Jeanette, but he had no interest in being at the Reed home again.

For the summer Jeanette had a job in the county welfare department. Happy that she had successfully completed her freshman year, she was proud of the school whose spirit seemed to fill her. She was glad that David had finished his work at Central and that he would have scholarship help in going on to State College. She acted as though David should have expected nothing less.

"I don't know what you've been worrying about," she said. "All your talk about trouble and bad feeling, I just don't see it. Even with some bad spots I can see things are getting better here, and this is a typical American city. It's really everybody's town."

After his graduation David went to work full time for Sam at the hardware store. His pay was less than it had been when he worked on the clean-up crew at Foundation the summer before, but it was regular. He learned the work and proved to be an invaluable employee. He could cut glass now as well as the older men. He could thread pipe, and he could do most of the work on aluminum doors and windows.

It was hot in June.

With the closing of school, children spilled into the streets. High school boys and girls scrambled for the few jobs available. David considered himself lucky. Many of his friends had nothing to do during the summer. The playgrounds and swimming pools started their programs, and the Carver Community Center had activities for all ages from preschoolers to senior citizens. Still, there were a lot of people who were idle. Some did not want to take regular organized activity just for the sake of keeping busy. Some could not find a place where they seemed to fit in.

The Park Department's swimming pools were crowded. The pools were not segregated. They were public facilities, and anyone could go to any pool. Just the same, the pool on the east side at Lincoln Park was the one that most colored people used. At the Highland Park pool in the northwest part of the city, colored people were never seen. There was no law against it. There was not even an unwritten rule. The park was in an area where only white people lived, and colored people stayed away from it.

At the pool in Stanton Park some colored swimmers could be found. David had never been there, but he knew others who had. Maybelle Reed and some of her friends on the west side often went to Stanton. They said that it was usually not crowded and the white kids didn't bother them.

But David had heard that there had been incidents of name-calling and ugly remarks at Stanton, sometimes in the locker rooms and sometimes going in and out. However, he had never heard of any real fights.

That is, he had never heard of any real fights before the summer of the riot. It was at the Stanton Park pool that the trouble started.

Maybelle Reed and Jeanette Lenoir had gone together to Stanton Park that Saturday. Jeanette later told David that when they arrived, a little after one o'clock, the place was already crowded. It was a very hot day. They had gone in, keeping rather close together, though not because they thought of being in danger. They were quite accustomed to having boys make fly remarks, but these they could handle.

There were no older colored boys at the pool that day. A dozen or more little boys and girls were playing with the usual noisy romping.

As at any pool, the youngsters were constantly involved in chases and duckings with loud talk and shouting and screaming. No one was disturbed by the activity. There was little cause for concern. It was a normal day.

At about three o'clock Jeanette was sitting by the pool at the four-foot level with her feet in the water. Maybelle was lying on the pavement beside her. Maybelle had oiled her skin, saying, "I don't mind tanning, but I don't like to burn."

Jeanette laughed. "I don't burn, and I don't tan," she said, "I just get blacker. That's all. I just get blacker."

"But you've got the kind of skin that can take it," Maybelle said, shaking the hair from in front of her face. "When you get darker, you still look good, maybe even better. When I burn, I just look awful—red and splotchy and sick."

Then Jeanette saw a crowd chasing a couple of little colored boys at the deep end. There was a scuffle. First one child, then the other, was thrown in the water. At the time she thought they must be friends.

Then Maybelle spoke to her, asking her to rub her back with the tanning oil, and Jeanette complied. At the same time she heard a lifeguard's whistle and saw some activity. That was not unusual. The lifeguard was leading someone away with a crowd of others following behind. They went off toward the locker room.

It must have been a half hour later that people started to run and point. A lifeguard came down from the tower. There were more excited gestures. Soon the lifeguard came up from the water, holding the form of a black child. People ran, Jeanette among them. At poolside they gave artificial respiration. Mechanical respirators were used. More colored youngsters gathered around.

It was too late. The boy was dead.

Jeanette only thought that it was a very horrible accident.

Then she remembered the two little boys who had been chased and thrown into the deep end. Perhaps this was one of them.

"Why," she asked herself, "why when I saw that those colored kids were thrown in did I not make sure that they could swim and get safely out?"

She was ashamed. She felt it was her fault as much as anyone else's. She knew how people played at a swimming pool, and she knew that these two youngsters might have been terrified. Perhaps they could not swim at all. Perhaps as their bodies arched through the air, both of them were fearful that this would be the end. Perhaps those who had thrown them in were indifferent to the fact they could not swim. Perhaps they had not noticed whether they came out of the deep water or not. In fact, they could not have stayed to notice whether they had.

The boy who was drowned lived on the west side. His father, like David's father, was employed at the Foundation Iron and Machine Works and he, too, had been laid off.

David heard about the matter just before six o'clock as the hardware store was closing.

"They killed another one of our people at Stanton Pool today," John Bowman said to him. "How long is this thing going to go on?"

He told David that there was to be a meeting of the brotherhood and urged David to attend.

David hurried home. He knew Jeanette had planned to go to the Stanton Park pool that afternoon. He telephoned her to find out what she knew.

"I guess I feel that I'm to blame, too," Jeanette said. "I noticed when they threw those kids in the water, and I should have been watching to see if they got out. It was the deep end. I guess I just didn't think."

"You've got no cause to blame yourself," David said. "You just don't know, you can't imagine, how mean some of them are."

"No, it wasn't meanness. They were playing. They were just playing."

David talked to Jeanette a little longer. He then called John Bowman and reported what she had said.

"Yes, playing! Having a little fun! And not caring if a black child is killed. They just don't care," Big John said.

David decided to go over to the east side. He wanted to see what was going on. He father was out with the car, so he decided to take the bus. As he rode, he thought he might even go to the brotherhood meeting.

It was a warm summer evening, not yet dark. People were out on the streets. They seemed to be excited. Many of them were angry. He left the bus at Fifth and Broad, and started walking out toward the house where the brotherhood would meet.

People were gathering in clusters. The clusters were merging into crowds. In each crowd one or two men were talking louder than the others, protesting what the whites were doing. Over and over, David heard the question, "How long are we going to take it?"

On Saturday night the stores usually stayed open late, but this evening some of the stores and shops were already closed and locked; others were being shut. At the

Emporium Department Store a uniformed security guard stood in the door, barring the way with his club. He lifted it like a gate for those who were leaving, but he allowed no one to enter.

David stopped at the edge of one of the larger crowds. He listened to the man standing on the curb, haranguing the throng.

"Black man has been taking it too long," shouted the man, and many around him in the street and on the sidewalk shouted in approval.

"The white man thinks we got no feelings. He thinks we'll just go on taking anything he puts on us. He thinks we don't care, 'cause we been grinning and bearing it. We been waiting for some kind of pie in the sky."

"Ain't it the living truth!" someone called.

"White man thinks black mothers don't love their little children, and that's 'cause black mothers leave their own young ones dirty, playing in the street, and go wash the white man's children and cook for them and clean up their houses."

"That's another God's truth," was one of the supporting cries.

"White man thinks the black man don't love the black woman, else the black man wouldn't let his woman leave his home to go and serve the white man just any way the white man wants."

In the crowd emotions were rising with the fervor of the speaker. Men and women were shouting with him, echoing, approving.

A woman with a baby in her arms cried out, "Tell it like it is, good brother! Tell it like it is!"

Another woman, an older, heavier woman, screamed, "That could have been my child killed today."

"They say the black man is happy. They say 'Look at him; see him dancing; hear him laughing; listen to his songs; he's got to be happy.'

"Well it's time to tell it like it is. We got to make them know the truth.

"They're doing it in other places. Folks are speaking up. They're saying, 'We're done with laughing for you! We're done with crawling and with begging! We're standing up like free-born men, Americans.'

"Maybe you all here are satisfied. They tell me this is a white man's town. They say ain't nothing we can do here."

A hand fell on David's shoulder. It was Jimmy Hicks. David stepped back, away from the speaker, to greet his friend.

"It's rough, man," Jimmy said. "Everybody's fed up."

They started walking, exchanging ideas, agreeing that the whites were bearing down harder and harder on the blacks and that something had to be done about it.

Jimmy complained about his own difficulties. He hadn't been able to get what he called a halfway decent job.

"Experience! They say I need experience! But how I going to get that experience if they won't let me work?"

David saw that although Jimmy looked clean, his clothes were shabby. His knitted polo shirt was torn. His sneakers had burst out at the sides and they were not laced to the top. His hair was "natural"—not only had it not been cut for a long time but it had not been combed.

David felt sorry for him. When he saw Jimmy fishing

in his breast pocket, David took out his own pack of cigarettes and offered him one. Jimmy accepted gladly.

They had to raise their voices to hear each other over the noise of the crowd. All about them people were shouting and talking. More and more everyone seemed to agree: "Somebody ought to do something."

"They're taking on white boys to train to take over jobs like your old man had," Jimmy said bitterly. "Them cats don't need experience. All they need to be is white."

Over the sound of excited talk, the blare of radios and loudspeakers, another sound could be heard in the air. It had a beat, a rhythm with many voices.

A mass of people was approaching, moving westward slowly down the street. They were walking hard, stomping. Some were waving pieces of wood and metal, carrying them like clubs. One phrase came from them over and over: "Stanton Park! Stanton Park! Stanton Park!"

As they drew near, David could see that most of them were boys, young boys in their teens. One was rapping out the rhythm on a bottle. Another was beating on the lid of a garbage can. Beside him David heard Jimmy take up the cry: "Stanton Park! Stanton Park! Stanton Park!"

The first of the stomping crowd went by, and then older boys and men were passing. As they passed, others stepped out from the sidewalk to the street to join the movement. Head was among those in the throng. He beckoned with a wide swing of his arm, and Jimmy said, "Let's go, man! Let's go!"

David, feeling like a swimmer who had stood on the bank too long, stepped out. He, too, took up the cry:

"Stanton Park! Stanton Park! Stanton Park!" He raised his hand over his head, clenched in a hard fist. He was one with the crowd, screaming with excitement, with anger, with the thought of an eight-year-old black boy drowned by white people at a public pool.

The cry of "Stanton Park! Stanton Park! Stanton Park!" went on, but other things were also being shouted, some of them repeated over and over, and all of them sounding together made one united roar.

"Let's go, man! Let's go!"

"Make them know how it feels! Make them know how it feels!"

"We ain't taking it no more! We ain't taking it no more!"

David was swept along. He was no longer thinking as David Andrew Williams. He was scarcely thinking.

At the same time he knew that it was crazy. It was crazy and it was evil. Yet he felt it was necessary, and he was glad he was in it, moving forward, as part of it, one of the angry ones in the street.

"Stanton Park! Stanton Park! Stanton Park!"

The shouts he heard, the movements and the emotions of those about him, released in him a flow of being, unchecked by thought or reason.

Nothing was holding him back. If anyone had asked whose side he was on, he would have answered that he was on the side of his people.

If anyone had asked, "Whose town is this?" he would have shouted back, "It's everybody's town, but they're trying to make it a white man's town."

If they had asked, "Who is it you're trying to protect?"

he would have said, "Little boys going swimming and men like my father, laid off and getting mean and losing heart, and decent fine women like my mother, going out to work and getting fired for speaking the truth. I'm trying to protect all of us.

"Our town, man! Everybody's town!"

Before they reached Main Street, they heard the sound of sirens and ahead of them they saw the flashing lights of police cars. Young boys had been in the front of the line. Now older, stronger men moved forward. Beside a car parked in the middle of the street, with its red and orange lights flashing, a policeman was urging them to disband. Nobody in the crowd listened. They only moved on, and the car was soon in the middle of a sea of screaming, enraged faces. Another police officer in the car was talking rapidly into his microphone.

At Main Street the way was blocked by police cars. The crowd stopped for a while. A police officer, with gold on his sleeve and on his cap, talked to them through his bull horn. The crowd had to stop because they could not get through. The voice of the police was booming at them with orders to disperse. Some in the crowd shouted back in defiance. They reviled and cursed and threatened the police. Louder than anything else was the chant—now almost a roar—coming over and over from men and boys, and from the high-pitched voices of women, too: "Stanton Park! Stanton Park! Stanton Park!"

At the roadblock of cars, the police began making a stand, trying to stop the onward movement of the crowd. They used their clubs, but with the force of numbers the marchers were pressing on. Some went down with broken heads, but the sight of blood only excited those who came up behind. Policemen lost their clubs; the marchers fought back, and they kept advancing. David had no stick or weapon, but he forced his way on; he kept going forward, in the way Coach Henderson had taught him, "You don't stop. You keep going forward. You don't ever stop."

A little way off to one side, Jimmy Hicks was waving one of the clubs the police had lost. With this he was advancing.

The front of the crowd was sweeping up and over the cars of the police; the officers themselves were retreating, trying to protect themselves with whatever order they could maintain.

Jimmy Hicks, holding the night stick now in both hands, set upon the car nearest him. His teeth were clenched. Blow after blow came down: windshield, side windows, lights, everything that was glass he attacked. Others struck passing blows at the car, thumping the hood, the fenders, the top of the trunk. No one else in the crowd stayed by the car long. Jimmy seemed determined to wreck it completely. He stopped and backed away and returned again, striking with thrusts this time, poking out even the small jagged triangles of glass from around each opening.

Beyond the line of cars more and more police cars were rolling in, each spilling out its load of helmeted, club-swinging men. The police fought their way forward. Those who were near them could not fall back because of the pressure of those behind. The police could not get through. Heads were being cracked. People were going down. Men were fighting back. And always there were shouts—and more sounds of breaking glass. Things were flying through the air, and then David heard the cry, "Fire." As he looked back, he saw on one side of the street a dim, flickering light. It flamed and became brighter. On the other side of the street, equally dim and flickering at first, there were other lights. He knew that buildings were being set afire. He was in the middle of a riot, a riot of angry people. Sirens were sounding. The crowd was still moving forward, and over and around the police cars. All the cars were being smashed.

The cry of Stanton Park was no longer in the air. People were shouting, "This is it," and, "Watts in North Town."

The crowd could no longer move forward. More police cars came. With their cars they threw up a second, solid road block. They were helped by the firemen with their hook-and-ladder trucks. The firemen could not get through with their trucks, but they did get hoses hooked up, and they worked the lines forward through the crowd toward the fires that were burning now on both sides of the street. Those who were in the area got wet. They shouted their defiance and screamed their hate. But they could no longer move forward.

Gradually the crowd fell back. The people began moving toward the east side. They left behind a block of stores and business places about half of which had been smashed open and several of which had burned. Merchandise was strewn in the street. Some of it was carried away by looters. David could not tell how many had been arrested. Some who had been hurt were carried off in ambulances and police cars. Others whose heads were bruised and whose faces were bloody were helped away by friends.

By midnight the streets were fairly well cleared. Whatever traffic moved was driven with great care. All of the police in the area, all the city firemen and state highway patrolmen, were on duty.

It was after twelve o'clock when David, who had reached the Community Center, tried to telephone his parents. The line was dead.

David was anxious to get home. People in the lobby were clustered about radios, listening to the reports. David knew his parents would have heard about the riot and that they would be frightened. He hoped his father would not decide to drive in the car to find him. He did not yet dare start walking homeward. He feared arrest. He feared he would be attacked by white men if he once got into the area where there were few colored people. Those colored people who moved on the streets were going in spurts from one house to the next. Police cars with their spotlights on were cruising through the district. Officers in white helmets rode in them, their shotguns at the ready.

A car with a loudspeaker was coming down the street, moving slowly. David and others listened. The voice was familiar. Someone was asking the people to clear the streets and return to their homes and restore order. It was a plea for reason. David listened for the words.

There was a pause and then it started over. "This is Reverend Samuel Hayes, your pastor at First Baptist

Church," David heard. "I implore you in the name of God, give up the violence and reckless action that has torn us this night. Violence begets violence, and hate begets hate. We are striking blindly, and we aren't hurting our true enemies or removing the real dangers. We are often striking at friends and those who are already on our side. The price that we will pay will be heavy. It will be in our own loss of self-respect. I implore you in the name of God to stay in your homes until the morning and then gather in houses of prayer and seek God's direction. This is Samuel Hayes, your pastor . . ."

"That's all well and good for the preacher to say," Head said to David, "but the Reverend Moshombo tells it different. He says God is just as angry at white folks as we are. He says that God is a mighty man of war, and sometimes you have to go out and fight."

"But I still wonder if maybe the Reverend Hayes isn't right," David argued. "Our people smashed in some windows, and they set some fires. Were these the enemies that we were to attack?"

Jimmy Hicks said, "Well, I know I feel better now. I do know I feel better."

And Head said, "Blood's thicker than water, and when it really gets tight, all the whites go together. That's why all the blacks got to go together, too. Then we can have it out."

"That's what I used to think. Especially that's what I used to think when I was down South. Now I know like the old white man said one night down there when there was trouble, 'It ain't every white man that's against colored folks.' "

They talked a while, arguing at times. Trying to understand. They spoke of "getting even" and of their rights.

Big John Bowman joined them.

"We just heard from the Reverend Moshombo," he said excitedly. He's in New York, but he's coming to North Town—he'll be in tomorrow. He knows what's going on. We'll be having a big meeting as soon as he gets here."

"What do you think he'll say?" Head asked.

"Can't tell yet. He'll be here tomorrow. Tell everybody."

As Big John Bowman started off, happy and excited, to tell others his news, David called after him. "How about giving me a lift home?"

John turned and came back. "You live over on the west side, don't you?" he said. "I don't know if I dare drive over that way. The whites are liable to be out with guns. Wouldn't want to have any bad trouble with them."

"Maybe we could get a police car to escort us," David said.

"Help from them?" John made a sweeping motion with his hands, and he and Head and Jimmy laughed. "Help from them white cops? That *would* be asking for trouble. Only way we could make it would be to keep away from them, 'cause if they even so much as see us we would be in trouble."

David did not agree, but he would not argue. John left after saying he would see what he could do for him.

David again tried to telephone his home. On the first ring his father answered the phone.

"I'm all right. I'm at the Community Center . . ." David

told him. "No, I don't want you to come after me. . . . It might be dangerous, but I'll be home after a while. . . . No, tell Mom not to worry about me. . . . Well, just tell her that I'm all right, that I haven't been in any trouble. I saw what was going on, but I didn't do anything."

He thought of calling Jeanette. Everyone at the Lenoir house would be up and awake; Jeanette might be worried about him. He decided against it.

John Bowman came back with another man to where David was standing. "This is Brother Randle who lives over your way," he said. "He wants to go home, and he thinks he can make it. So he can take you with him and drop you off on his way."

David started to express his thanks, but John cut in, to give them very definite instructions:

"Now look," he said. "You may get stopped by somebody. That's the chance it looks like you want to take. But you got to decide right here and now whether you're going to be nonviolent or fight back."

Randle said that he had nothing to fight back with and he had no intention of putting up any resistance to the police or even to a mob of whites. David, too, said he was willing to take his chances. He had no weapon; he just hoped there would be no necessity to fight.

"Well, that's it then," John said, acting like a commandant. "If the police stop you, you just got to talk to them and let them know that you live over there and you're on your way home. If whites get after you, maybe you can speed off, but I just hope that don't happen."

Randle was not talkative, and David was anxious not

to prolong the conversation. About all that Randle said was "It just don't make sense."

As they left the Carver Community Center and drove westward with Randle at the wheel, David realized that the east side had become quiet. The acrid smell of smoke hung in the air.

Randle drove very carefully, making all necessary stops and approaching each intersection with care. Police cars were moving about with their radio speakers blasting. People stood outside their doors, and some stood at the street corners, but few pedestrians were to be seen. Randle avoided driving through the block where property had been damaged.

Main Street was brightly lighted, and they noticed activity there. As they rode west into the residential neighborhood, there were lights on in almost every home. Garage and porch lights were bright, and cars were moving on the streets. Men were walking about with clubs and with guns. Some of them were wearing helmets. All the people they saw were white. There were no women in sight.

The cars here moved more swiftly. Randle, not wanting to draw attention to himself, began to drive faster, but he slowed carefully at every crossing. When David left the car in front of his own home, Randle had only two more blocks to go, and both of them felt that there would be no danger now.

Inside the house, David's family was watching television in the living room. They had been watching it since eight o'clock, seeing pictures of the riot, of the stores on fire and pictures televised from police headquarters and hospitals. They asked David questions faster than he could answer them.

He wanted to tell them just how it had been. He found it hard to explain. He really did not know what had been in people's minds. He could not say what the crowd planned to do if it reached Stanton Park. In fact, he was sure there was no plan. Perhaps the people just wanted to express themselves, just make a demonstration, but he was not sure what it was they wanted to express or what the demonstration would prove.

His mother excused herself, saying that she had promised to call the Lenoirs as soon as David came in.

His father asked him more questions.

David was still shaking with excitement and fear that had engulfed him in the crowd. It was literally sending spasms of trembling through his body. Out in the street he had believed he had the answers. Now, seated in his own home, with his father pacing back and forth in front of him, David had no easy answers.

"I'd be the first to admit," his father said, "that it's hard for the colored man. It's hard all over, down South and up North, too. And it's hard to know that our young ones are not protected in a public park. But I still say that trying to pull down the whole house over your head just don't make sense. True, I'm out of a job, but it's true, too, that I had a job, and I'll be back on the job, or some kind of job, most any day now. That is, I'll be back on the job if the man don't say we can't use no more colored because colored burn up and fight and destroy. They might say that. Anybody that looks at those pictures on TV tonight will say it. And they'll think that everybody is in it. And it don't do me no good to think that my own son was in that crowd."

"But, Dad, I didn't do anything. I was there, but I didn't do anything."

"How long does it take you to learn that when you're there you are a part of it? Looks like by now you would know that. Have you got to be witness to more killing? Haven't you had enough? And suppose you'd been arrested? You know what's hanging over your head."

"Yes, I know," David spoke slowly. "I know. I thought about it, and didn't care."

On television the late show had been replaced by live coverage of the events of the day and the night. A member of the City Council was being interviewed:

"With the mayor out of town, I took the liberty of phoning the governor's office. I have demanded that they send in the National Guard. Law and order have been challenged. Those people are going crazy, it looks like. They're trying to take over the town. The chief of police is efficient and completely competent. He has a fine corps of officers, and they have done splendidly. But we can't tell how much farther this thing is going to go. This is just the beginning; it's going to get worse, I know."

"It don't have to get worse," David's father said, "but if that kind of talk keeps on, it will get worse."

The councilman went on to say that the citizenry would have to protect itself. He asked that all law-abiding citizens recognize their responsibilities to keep the peace, but that keeping the peace might come to the point of sharing in the protection of their homes. He urged merchants and storekeepers to be very sure to sell firearms only to law-abiding citizens who would use them only for protection, not for attack. He said there were some law-abiding Negro citizens, too, and he wanted to assure them that they would be protected, but that they must be careful not to become involved in the rioting. Then he proposed a plan:

"I have a plan for all you law-abiding Negroes who want to join in it for your own safety," he said. "You can express your willingness to cooperate and you will receive the protection that you deserve. I ask you to hang out of your windows white cloths, sheets, or towels—or anything that will let the law-abiding citizens of this city know that you want to be on their side. If our citizens and our armed police and servicemen do not see by this sign that you are on the right side, they will have to presume that you are unwilling to cooperate and you will have to suffer the consequences."

Mr. Williams was not a man to talk loosely and to use profanity in front of his family, but this time he did. With an oath, he stamped his foot. "I'm not going to run up any white flag!" he shouted. "If that's the way it's got to be, surrender to a white mob, then I guess we just have to face it. God knows we faced it down South, and I didn't come North to surrender.

"I won't go off the premises to attack nobody," he added. "I won't go out to get in a fight, but if any man comes here to harm my family, I'll blow his head off. So help me God, I will."

Mrs. Williams from the kitchen called to David to come and eat. But David did not want to leave the television set. Other speakers were coming on, and there were flashbacks of scenes in the street.

"I made some coffee," Mrs. Williams said at the door. "The Lenoirs always drink coffee when they come over, no matter what time it is. You all better come and get something."

Neither David nor his father left the living room; they wanted to see and to hear. After calling them a second time, Mrs. Williams brought sandwiches and coffee on a tray. David was glad to get them. He was hungry.

David's father told him that he had put his shotgun and David's rifle, cleaned and oiled, near the upstairs front window. He hoped there would be no trouble, no attacking by crowds of whites. He believed that it might be not too different from the way it was in the South. Mobs there did not attack people who were armed. They struck only when they knew their victims could not protect themselves.

"I guess even the worst of them," he said, "even the meanest rebels, don't hate so much that they want to die to prove it. They won't come on if they think they're going to get hurt."

David remembered a terrible night in the South. It was the family's last horrible experience before they moved North.

His father had been arrested. He had been arrested because he refused to accept helper wages from an employer who wanted him to work as a mechanic. He had refused and he had argued. It was the talking back that had angered the white man in South Town. Williams had been arrested. He had been beaten while he was in jail. A mob had come to the Williams's home, expecting to burn it in order to teach colored people to stay in what was called their place.

But the colored people had gotten together with guns, and they had laid in wait for the planned attack. Two white friends had come and joined them. When the mob arrived, one of the white men shouted in warning. He let the night riders know that those in the house would fight back and that he would be fighting on their side.

"There ain't going to be no house burning here tonight," he had said. "Clear out now! Clear out!"

David could still hear the words as though they had just been spoken. He had not thought of them for a long time.

The old man had said, "Get on back to your homes and your womenfolk while you're able, and come sunup look on the day and thank God you're living and beg Him to forgive you. Leave these people be. This here's Sam McGavock talking sense to you, and by God, I mean it."

They had driven away, four or five carloads of them. They had driven away, and after they left, those in the house relaxed. They had thought their vigil was over. They felt exhausted. It was like the end of a long day of working in the fields from sunup to sundown. They had relaxed too soon.

The night riders came back, driving swiftly and firing as they passed. The rattle of their guns, the splintering of wood and shattering of glass in the house, the angry curses of men taken off their guard, were over in seconds. When they made a light, they found one of the men was dead.

David remembered that night in all its horrible detail.

Betty Jane lay asleep on the couch. David and his father continued to watch the television screen. More interviews were shown. The chief of police reported that the situation was in hand but his force was prepared for trouble. He said he did not know how many had been arrested, but later a reporter stated that more than a hundred had been jailed. Two Negroes were dead. Many had been treated for wounds and bruises, most of them sustained in resisting arrest. The chief of police asked that people stay off the streets and out of the sensitive area, but the reporters spoke about indignant law-abiding citizens who were arming and organizing patrols. Nothing more was said about colored people hanging out white flags.

The Lenoirs had still not arrived.

"I guess they just changed their minds," Mr. Williams said. "Better they shouldn't be out on the street now anyway."

"But they said they were coming," Mrs. Williams replied. "I hope they're all right."

"Oh they're all right." Mr. Williams seemed very sure. "They just decided not to come, that's all. They just changed their minds when they heard all the talk about those folks acting like patterollers."

"Like what?" David asked.

"Patterollers," his father said, and repeated, "Patterollers."

David thought his father was trying to say "patrollers," but his father insisted Patterollers was the word he meant; it had been used by slaves before the Civil War.

White men, many of them poor whites, would watch the roads for runaway slaves, he explained. They made money by claiming rewards, but these small amounts never satisfied them. So they began to steal slaves, kidnapping the unwary and hustling them across state lines to sell them at bargain rates. They also would capture free Negroes, destroy their identification papers, and ship them by reverse underground railway to the deep South.

"Down home the old folks used to talk about them all the time," Mr. Williams concluded. "I don't see how you missed knowing about Patterollers."

At three o'clock the television station signed off. David's mother got Betty Jane up from the couch and led her to bed. David said he would wait awhile, maybe the Lenoirs would come after all. His father said, "They just changed their mind, that's all." And he went to bed.

David turned on the radio. He could not locate a news broadcast, so he got some music and sat thinking.

He thought about that terrible night in the South. When it was over, people had had to figure things out; they had to make plans. Now, on this night in North Town, he knew there must be many other Negroes who were trying to figure out what they had done and what they were going to do.

The Williams family had moved away from the South. At that time David hated white people. That is, he hated most of them. The few he did not hate he thought of as very unusual people. He considered the world of white people a world of enemies. Most of his friends felt the same way.

His experiences at Central High School in North Town had changed his attitude. A football player, Michael O'Connor, became his friend, and Mike taught David enough football to enable David to make the team. But there were colored students at the school who continued to hate white people. On the team David had learned, with Henderson as coach, that it mattered very little to most players what David's color was. Perhaps one or two of them were spiteful or mean, but this could have been just because David was a new man.

The first time he made a touchdown run he felt that he was really part of the team, part of the school, and part of the United States of America. It was the first time he had ever had such a feeling. It was not the last. Soon he just went along with that good feeling, not even thinking about it.

David knew something of the history of Negroes in America. In the colored school that he had attended in the South, there were exercises and programs around Negro History Week, which came in February. From the beginning, people of his race had shared in the making of America. They had fought in large numbers in every war, and black men had spilled their blood to make America great. In a more recent past he had known fellows just a little older than he was who had gone off to fight. Some of them had not come back; they had died fighting for what is known as democracy.

David stood up and drew his wallet from his hip pocket. He took out his draft card. He read again the words there. Then he went through the hall to the front door. As he opened the screen and walked out on the porch, he knew he was looking at America.

America was his country. He would deny that it was a white man's country. He knew that he had every right to claim first-class citizenship. He knew, too, that when Negroes were denied the rights of first-class citizenship this was done by persons within the country and not by the nation itself. Someday he might be called into military service. He would go because it would be fighting for his own country. He was American. There were Americans with white skins and Americans with black skins.

"All of us are Americans," he said as he walked back into the house and stretched out on the sofa. But if black men fought against white men and white men attacked black men, he wasn't sure what he should do.

There were those who believed that all the white people would stick together and that all black people should cling together and that the struggle was between white and black. It seemed otherwise to him. He knew that many white people were taking a stand with colored people. They were fighting for what they considered right. Perhaps, too, as on his football team, they were fighting for the whole of America.

Perhaps, he thought, that is it. Perhaps the answer to Lonnie Webster's question, "Whose side are you on?" was not so difficult after all.

When he played football for Central High School, he

knew whose side he was on. With him were ten other players who made up the team. Perhaps all of them were white. Sometimes there was one other colored player. Maybe they played against a team on which there were three, or four, or even more, colored players. So whose side was he on in the football game? Of course, he was on Central's side.

No matter what color the other team's players were, there would be no question of his going over and saying, "All us colored boys got to be on one team."

The very idea made him smile. "Hi, soul brother! You're supposed to let me get through."

So what about the nation? Well, that wasn't quite as simple. Out there in the night colored people battled against the police. But, after all, the police were not all white men. On whose side were Sergeant Reed and the other colored officers? Certainly they would have been on the side of the policemen. So again it was not a question of black and white. Then should he side with people of his own color, or should he side with the community? Should he side with America? Should he take his stand with the side that was right? Should he consider which side was right or should he consider only which side was black?

No, this matter of whose side you are on was not as simple as a football team. On the football team the sides were plainly marked. The men were marked by the positions they took at the beginning of the game and by the uniforms they wore. They worked together and they trained together as a unit. Out there in the streets, it wasn't like that. The one common bond out there was the color of the skin.

He would have to think about it some more. He would have to talk with some other people. He had to find out about this. It was important. The broadcasts had said that the trouble wasn't over yet. And if the trouble wasn't over, he still had to know whose side he was to be on.

Daylight came. David sat up with a start. He knew he had been asleep. Looking at his watch, he saw that it was after five in the morning. He turned off the radio. The Lenoirs had not come.

He went to the front door again and stepped out on the wide porch. In the east the sun was rising. It was just coming up over the tops of the houses. There was no smoke. The air was fresh and clean. Perhaps the terror and fear of the night before were over. He certainly hoped they were. There was nothing for him to do. He went indoors and made his way upstairs to his own room. There he quickly undressed and was soon asleep.

Nine

David wakened to find Betty Jane shaking him as he lay on his bed. The shades were raised; the room was flooded with sunlight.

"You got to get up, David," Betty Jane was saying. "We're going to church. You have to go, too. Everybody's going to church today. It's all on the radio. Everybody's supposed to go to church."

David had avoided going to church lately. For a while he had served as a junior deacon; he had ushered and helped to take up the collection. Now he was a member of the First Baptist Church but one of the many who seldom attended. He had also sung in the choir for a short time, but that duty required regular Thursday night attendance for rehearsal. He had to drop it.

As he stretched and yawned, Betty Jane told him

excitedly that the radio announcers were urging all citizens to go their houses of worship. Ministers had come on the air and urged everyone, white and colored, to join in prayer.

"I don't need to go to a prayer meeting," David said. "A prayer meeting would be all right if you got the right folks inside to pray. The trouble is, the folks that are going to be on the inside, they weren't doing anything anyway."

"Everybody's suppose to go," Betty Jane insisted.

"But everybody won't go," David answered.

He knew it was time to get dressed, that is, if he was to go to church. Anyway, he thought, it's not a bad idea, so he got up and went to the bathroom. He was in the shower when there was a loud knock on the door. His father put his head in the door.

"Dave, we can't get anybody over at the Lenoirs," Mr. Williams said. "We been trying to get them on the phone, and don't get any answer. When they didn't come over here last night, we thought it was because they'd decided not to leave the house."

"They must be there," David said. "Unless maybe they left early to go to Mass."

His father seemed satisfied and closed the door. David heard him going downstairs.

The Lenoirs were Roman Catholics. They had brought their religion with them when they moved from New Orleans. David knew that Jeanette often went to early Mass. If people were being urged to go to their houses of worship, they would surely go to Saint Dominica's.

At breakfast his mother said that the missionary sisters

of the First Baptist Church were telephoning all the members, asking them to come to church today. She supposed the Methodists and the Catholics were going to church, too.

"I never did understand how colored people could be Catholic," she said as she put two hot biscuits from the oven on the side of David's plate, already crowded with fried eggs, pork sausage, and applesauce.

"They say that in New Orleans lots of colored people are Catholic," David said.

"They tell me that with them the priest has to do all the praying," Mrs. Williams said.

David laughed. "Don't our folks always say, 'Pray for me, and I'll be praying for you,' or 'You ought to be praying for Brother so-and-so or Sister so-and-so?' "

"Oh, but that's different. After all, each of use can pray. We don't have to depend on the preacher or some priest."

"Well, maybe the preachers and priests stand a little closer to God, and maybe they think in the Catholic Church that God will hear them when he won't hear us miserable sinners."

David had talked with Jeanette about their differences in religion, but he admitted he understood very little of it. He settled the discussion by saying, "Anyway, I suppose it's mainly just a question of what you're used to. If a person is born in a home where the folks are Catholic and grows up that way, then he'll be Catholic. Maybe I ought to be glad my folks were born Baptist." He recited a little rhyme that Baptist children used to say when they taunted the children of other faiths:

"Baptist-born and Baptist-bred,
I'll be Baptist till I'm dead.
If you Methodist-born and Methodist-bred,
Supposed to be Methodist till you die,
But when old death comes knocking at the door,
Better jump over to the Baptist side."

The radio was loud with news. It was true that ministers and civic leaders were urging people to go to church, but the newscasters were saying over and over that the trouble had only just begun. They kept reporting things they had heard said the night before. A colored boy had said that Watts was coming to North Town and that by Sunday night everybody would know it. Each commentator picked up this remark and repeated it again and again.

David heard it on the car radio as he drove his family to church.

"Looks like them news people want to cause some more riot," his father said. "It's just like in the country when people are agitating two folks that really don't want to fight; they keep talking about what one fellow says he going to do. After a while the one they talking about has to do something to show he ain't scared. Keep talking about colored folks going to raise hell tonight, keep saying it's going to happen, what do they expect? They'll make it happen."

David agreed. He had seen what had happened the night before. He knew that most of the people in the street had not really been interested in creating a riot. They just found themselves sort of going along, the way he had—

not really doing anything, but being there to see what others were going to do.

They were approaching the block on Fifth Street where most of the damage had been done. Police barricades were up, and they had to detour. The acrid smell of smoke and burning wood and wet mortar was strong. Policemen and firemen with equipment were in the block. It looked as though some places were still smoldering.

"Now, that is a shame," Mrs. Williams said. "It's a shame, and it's not necessary. I don't know what they think they are going to get out of it."

The announcements broadcast over radio and television seemed to have had some effect on the town. The east side was quiet. Many people stood on the sidewalks and many others stood in their doorways, talking back and forth, discussing what they had seen and what they had heard in the past twenty-four hours. As the car approached the First Baptist Church, David realized he was in the middle of a traffic problem. It was difficult to find a parking place near the building. David let the others out and then drove on to find a space. When he returned, he saw others also hurrying. They were dressed in their Sunday best, but they looked worried. They seemed to be far removed from the thought of rioting.

As David entered the church, he saw that his family were already seated, though not in their usual place. Ushers were setting up folding chairs for the first time since Easter. This was not an Easter crowd, however. It seemed to be more like a funeral.

The choir had come in and the minister was reading

from the Bible. David's father squeezed over to make room for him at the aisle end of the pew.

The scholarly Reverend Hayes was reading from one of the familiar Psalms.

"In the time of trouble he shall hide me in his pavilion, in the secret of his tabernacle shall he hide me. Hide not thy face far from me; put not thy servant away in anger; thou hast been my help; leave me not, neither forsake me, O God of my salvation. . . .

"Deliver me not unto the will of mine enemies; for false witnesses are risen up against me, and such as breathe out cruelty. . . ."

David liked the way the minister's voice intoned the familiar, melodious phrases. It was almost as though he were chanting them.

"I had fainted, unless I had believed to see the goodness of the Lord in the land of the living."

The minister lifted his eyes from the Bible. As he looked out over the congregation he raised his hands in invitation and the people joined all together in the last verse:

"Wait on the Lord: Be of good courage, and he shall strengthen thine heart: Wait, I say, on the Lord."

The organist sounded a chord. A few latecomers found seats at the back of the auditorium. The choir chanted as the people bowed their heads. The minister prayed.

It was not a long prayer.

David remembered that he had not been in church since the day of Lonnie's funeral. He did not have a feeling of shame or guilt, but he was glad he was here this morning. In the midst of all the confusion and troubles of his own and of the community, he hoped that people in churches all over the city, white and black, might come to a better means of reaching agreement than by rioting with attacks and destruction of property. He hoped that perhaps he might be among those who would be a little better and have better understanding because of the prayer being offered.

In his sermon that morning the minister moved quickly from consideration of the Bible text to the problems of the day. He said that the laws of God are just as true and the power of God is just as great as it was two thousand years ago.

Then the pastor began to talk about race, specifically about Negroes and their attitude toward race. He spoke of things that David had just barely thought about. He had caught glimmers of them in some of the articles in *Ebony* magazine, and he had heard some of the ideas discussed on television by various national leaders. Still, the way the Reverend Hayes spoke this morning the ideas seemed to make more sense.

The minister said that a long time ago those who had promoted and profited by the institution of slavery had faced the challenge of decent people who opposed them and worked for abolition of the slave trade. Slave owners had given every possible reason for continuing the evil practice, and it was during this period that the great lie was established. The great lie, perhaps the greatest lie in all history, said: "These blacks from Africa are not really people, or if they are people, they are a sub-race. They are not capable of learning; they have no morals; they have no talents; they are, indeed, each and every one of them inferior beings who are better off in slavery than they could possibly be if they were freed from the control of their white owners."

He told them that even before the Civil War thousands of ex-slaves and their descendants had participated in American life as free men, that free black men had fought since the days of the Revolution in every war on the side of liberty and justice, to help establish and to maintain the United States. Eighty thousand free Negroes had enlisted during the Civil War. Paid at the rate of seven dollars a month while white soldiers were receiving thirteen, they said, "We will fight for nothing if necessary."

"After the Civil War," the Reverend Hayes went on to say, "the former slave owners in the South tried to maintain the great lie. Segregation, discrimination, terror, and every form of humiliation and bestiality were practiced on the former slaves to keep them in what was called 'their place.' And the warlord Hitler has made the world realize that if a lie is repeated often enough and loudly enough it will be believed."

So it was, he said, with the great lie. As Negroes were denied the fruits of their labor, denied education, denied the right to work for equal pay or to purchase and live in houses on the basis of their ability to own and maintain such property, as these limitations were systematically and even legally imposed, woefully and understandably Negroes themselves came to believe the great lie. Negro children looked about them and saw their parents living as second-class citizens. They saw the dilapidated schools in which they were taught, the cast-off books and discarded equipment from the white schools. They saw their fathers underpaid for their skills and their mothers forced to use the backdoors of white people when they went to scrub and clean homes that were not their own. These children grew to believe that it must be that the white people were superior. And if white people were superior, then, they concluded, black people must be inferior.

"America today pays a terrible price for the evil that has been done," said the Reverend Hayes. "Now we are involved in great conflicts all over the land. Negroes are in rebellion. They are striking back. They are trying to disprove the great lie. They are using many methods to advance the cause of real freedom. And I am one who says that we ought to struggle and fight toward full achievement as men and women, as citizens of America, as members of the great human race and children of God created in His own image."

The congregation responded with loud calls of "Amen" and, "Preach the word," and "Tell it like it is."

"But"—the minister lifted his hand and the audience quieted—"but, we must be wise. We must be wise, and we must be right. We are not wise, and we cannot be right if we operate on a false premise."

By this time David was leaning forward to catch each word. He was still trying to find the answer to his own questions. He thought maybe the minister—older, wiser, well educated and highly experienced—could give him a clue.

"First," the minister said, holding up one finger. "First we must recognize that the great lie was indeed a lie, that there are no superior or inferior races, that each one of us, that I and you and you and you, are individual persons. We know that some people have more ability than others but that this has nothing to do with the color of the skin. We know that each of us has more potential than is ever utilized, that each of us has moral and spiritual values, and that we ourselves must respect them.

"Second, we must realize that white people also are people, no better and at the same time no worse than colored people. And that within the body of the white race there are many—nay, millions—of people who are on the side of right. One of our great mistakes is to do what we accuse white people of doing. We are offended when white people say all colored people are the same. We must know that there is no such thing as 'the white man.' We say this as we also say there is no such thing as 'the Negro' or 'the black man.' There are white people, and there are black people, but we must not force white people into a stereotype as we would not ourselves be forced into a sterotype. All through history white people have died for freedom; many died for the freedom of black people during the Civil War. Many have gone to the ends of the earth, struggling and fighting to help people of color. We must recognize that many white people are actively and anxiously working to help us even today.

"Third, we must realize as we recognize our own manhood and womanhood that there are many people within our own ranks who are unwilling to sacrifice for freedom. Most people in this world—white, black, yellow, green, pink, or whatever—just want to be left alone. Most of us do not want to be disturbed. Most of us do not want to be crusaders or reformers. And this is not wrong. I say it, not as a criticism, but as a fact. And I must remind you that most white people are not interested in keeping Negroes down. Most of them simply do not care. Many white people are fearful. They consider the shouts of 'freedom now' and 'black power' as threats. They want to protect themselves, but most of them are not in opposition to the rights of other people who are not the same color. This has been demonstrated over and over again."

David thought of some of the white people he had known. There was Travis, who had died in South Town. There was old Mr. Mack. And there was Sam Silverman—well, Sam was a Jew, but he was still white. And there was Mike O'Connor who had helped him get on the football team. And there was Coach Henderson who certainly had tried to be fair, and then there was the other members of the team. He supposed that none of them had really tried to give him a hard time. And once he was there and had demonstrated that he could play and that he was willing to put his heart into the game they had all joined together in making a team.

The minister was talking about the song, "We Shall Overcome." He asked if the members of the congregation had ever seriously thought about the real meaning of its words.

He asked them what they were intending to overcome. Then he answered his own question, saying that he thought no one when they sang that song was thinking of winning a battle against people. The civil rights movement was not a movement of black people against white people. Rather it was a struggle of mankind to overcome evil and hate and selfishness.

"When we join hands and sing 'Black and White together, we shall overcome,' we are expressing the real meaning of the struggle.

"We shall not overcome by destroying property or by spilling the blood of others or by pouring out our own blood in suicidal sacrifice. We shall not overcome by filling the jails or the hospitals. We shall overcome by first recognizing truth and raising our heads, and moving forward in the sun, by recognizing our own manhood and strength and possibility and by exhibiting it and utilizing all of our forces. We shall overcome the indifference of others. We shall overcome as we recognize that those who oppose us do not have right on their side and that they are few in number indeed. We shall overcome with black and white together, not by demanding that God be on our side but by always making sure that we are on God's side. We shall overcome, and we shall be of good cheer, and we shall know that God has already provided us with all that we need—the strength, the courage, the power.

"Go down from this temple. Go out into the streets. Go out to your homes and to your shops and to your jobs and to your schools. Go out recognizing yourselves as children of God. Go out willing to struggle against evil and hatred and fear, but unwilling to support or endorse hatred and evil."

David felt himself to be at ease.

"This is it," he said softly.

TEN

AS DAVID LEFT THE CHURCH, he saw members of the brotherhood passing out handbills:

> "Monster Mass Meeting—The Voice from Africa—Reverend Prempey Moshombo—Peterman Park, 3:00 P.M.—Learn What Is Happening to You and What You Can Do about It."

Mr. Green recognized David and pressed forward toward him.

"Come on, Williams," he said. "You got to help us." He handed him some of the flyers.

For a moment David felt certain that he had no help to offer to Green and the brotherhood. But on second thought, when he remembered the words of the Reverend Hayes, he realized that Green and the other members of the brotherhood were truly in need of help. They were spreading hatred because they did not understand the real cause of their troubles. He wished that all of them had heard the positive exposition and logic of the minister in his sermon.

"Why don't you leave the boy alone?" David's father said, pushing himself between David and the older man. "He's in enough trouble already."

"I know the trouble he's in, and I'm in it, too, and so are you. We're all in it together, and now's the time to do something about it," Green said.

"You're right, man. It *is* time to do something." David saw that his father was becoming angry. "It's time to do something, but what you folks want to do is the wrong thing. You should have heard what the preacher said."

"Preacher talking about turning the other cheek and spilling our blood."

"It's not that! You don't know."

"Well, how many cheeks he think I got?"

Others had stopped to listen to the exchange. The two men were soon the center of a crowd of listeners. They had just come out of church, and they were still under the influence of the minister's preaching. During the service David had been very sure of where he stood. Now, listening to Green, he was less certain.

He heard his father say, "I've been in every kind of trouble that a black man has, and I've known the meanest white folks you can find, but I know all of them ain't like that, and that's what I want my boy to know."

Someone in the crowd—David could not see who it was—called out, "Uncle Tom."

A second man—and this time David could see that the speaker was a member of the brotherhood—shouted, "We fighting back, and if we die, we die like men."

Green continued to urge them to join with Moshombo.

Andy Crutchfield pushed his heavy bulk through the crowd. "Ed, Ed," he called out. "You're wasting your time talking with these people. They're full of the devil, just looking for trouble and trying to make trouble for everybody. You're wasting your time."

He took Mr. Williams by the arm and drew him away.

Green kept on talking, directing his words toward David. "Are you going to let those old handkerchief heads tell you what to do? You going to let the white folks rob you of your manhood? Ain't you got sense enough to see Prempey Moshombo is right?"

David had been thinking of replying to Green, but with that last question, he knew it was useless to answer. He shook his head and called to the others, "The car is in the next block."

Music sounded from the car radio as David turned on the switch. He waited for his father, who was talking excitedly to Andy Crutchfield. Slowly he moved across the dial, trying to get news. On WNOR he learned that the mayor was now back in the city, that the governor had called out the National Guard, and that two more of the injured had died. The prediction that Watts was coming to North Town was repeated.

The announcer was talking of other things when Mr.

Williams got in the car. David turned off the radio, turned on the ignition, and drove off.

"I hope it's over," his mother said. "I hope and pray there won't be any more. People like that man just don't make sense. Things are bad enough. They were bad down South. They don't get better by killing or getting killed."

"You hear what Andy said?" his father asked, and then went on. "He says Foundation's ready to call all the workers back. Orders are coming in. Notices are supposed to go out the first of July. You know what that will mean."

Even Betty Jane could understand. She said, "Then if people are working—all the colored people, I mean, who have been laid off—if they're working again, it won't be so bad."

David said, "I'll bet Mr. Green back there and the others haven't heard. Maybe we'd better go back and tell them."

"No, it's too soon for that," his father said. "After all, Andy just heard it, but still I'm sure it's true. Andy's been there a long time, and he knows a lot about what's going on."

David was driving south on Washington Street. At 18th Street Mrs. Williams said, "Why don't we go by and see the Lenoirs."

Everybody thought that was a good idea.

The Lenoir house seemed to be very quiet. David jumped out of the car and had started toward the door of the house when Mr. Lenoir opened the door and asked him to move the car into the driveway.

The news was bad.

Mrs. Lenoir and Jeanette were asleep. They had been

arrested, all of them, and had returned home only an hour ago.

There was terror and tension and bitterness and anguish and great pain in Mr. Lenoir's story.

After hearing that David was home, they had, indeed, started to drive to the Williams home. They were stopped on the street by young white men, cruising the area in two cars. While they were being held at gunpoint, questioned and searched and subjected to threats, profanity, and unprintable obscenities, a police car arrived on the scene. At first the Lenoirs had been glad to see the uniformed officers, but the only result of their presence was that the men with the guns became even more belligerent. It was as though their activities had the support of the law.

One of them said something obscene to Jeanette.

Mr. Lenoir stopped talking. His hands came up in fists. David felt his own muscles tighten. Mr. Lenoir was not a large man. He had always seemed to be gentle and completely in control of his temper. Now his words came through clenched teeth.

"I tried to kill him. They got me down. Beat me. Put handcuffs on me."

David could only imagine the details of the action. No one spoke. They just waited while Mr. Lenoir remembered, reviewing, perhaps, what he could leave out and what he had to tell. Betty Jane was standing beside her mother who was seated. The girl was crying.

"The jail was a madhouse. . . . packed in. Everybody angry, cursing. Most of them arrested for no good reason. Some had been hurt."

Mr. Williams said, "No, man. No." He bowed his head.

Mr. Lenoir went on as though he had not seen or heard:

"This morning—it must have been about nine o'clock—they started calling men out. I was one of the last. They asked a lot of questions—told me I was charged with resisting arrest, but that I could leave if I would sign an appearance bond. After that I had to stand in line to get information about my wife and Jeanette. They were locked up in the courthouse. It must have been even harder for them than it was for me."

"But they had each other," Mrs. Williams said. "I know they were worried about you, but they had each other. You were alone."

"I was alone? I was alone in a pack of madmen. And I guess I was just like the others. No better. We were all the same. Just black."

"Try to get some rest," Mr. Williams said. "Don't talk no more."

Mrs. Williams offered to stay at the Lenoirs' in case her help was needed, but Mr. Lenoir said they would be all right. He had a loaded gun in the house.

"Maybe later today we ought to check," said Mr. Williams. "This thing's not over."

So it was agreed.

For the rest of the day the members of the Williams family stayed at home, following events in the city on TV and on radio. Their telephone was busy. Lawyer Taylor's wife phoned, worried, saying that her husband was very busy but wanted to make sure that the Williamses were safe. Jimmy Hicks called. He said that his mother told him she was worried sick when he was out there, but that she was glad he had smashed the police car.

Becky Goldberg called.

"My folks have been worried about you," she told David. She started to question him about himself, his father, what the Williams family were doing. David had a feeling that he was being interviewed, but he answered her questions freely. He believed in Becky's sincerity.

When he began to tell her he had been in the riot area, she stopped him.

"Wait a minute! Hold it! Hold it!" she almost shouted.

When she came back on the line, she said, "Dave, my dad is listening on the extension. I want him to hear this, too."

She started her questions again. "Now you said you were on East Fifth Street last night. Will you tell us just what happened first?"

David thought for a moment. He told about the crowd of boys with the cry of "Stanton Park!"

"But why, Dave? Why this bit about Stanton Park?"

"Well that was where this kid was drowned, and the way Jeanette told me it really looked like a killing."

"A killing?" That was Mr. Goldberg's voice, and David started to explain. The voice interrupted again. "Who is this Jeanette that told you all this?"

Becky's voice: "Oh, I know her, Daddy. She used to go to Central. Smart girl. David's girlfriend, I guess."

David spoke again. "Yes. And did you know that Jeanette was one of those the police arrested last night? Jeanette and her father and mother. They're at home now. Nobody knows what will happen next."

Mr. Goldberg's voice: "Young man, I'd like to talk to you, and maybe to some of the others. How about? . . . Suppose I come to your house? . . . Would that be all right? . . . Do you think it would be safe?"

"Well, you'd be safe so far as our people are concerned," David said, annoyed that safety should have to be considered. "I don't know though about the white volunteers and the police. Some other time, maybe. It might not be safe just now."

After giving more information and promising to talk again soon, he turned from the phone and told his father of the call.

Mr. Williams warned that they ought to be careful.

"But we've got nothing to hide," David said. "And besides, everybody knows what kind of person Becky is, and her father must be the right kind, too. I think we can trust them."

During the afternoon the mayor spoke on TV. He appealed for order and reason, promising swift punishment to all lawbreakers and protection to the person and property of all decent, law-abiding citizens. He sounded less firm than the governor who had come to North Town from the capital.

In the late afternoon the Lenoirs arrived. Mrs. Lenoir and Jeanette had rested. They did not want to talk about what had happened to them.

Mr. Lenoir said, "North or South, we do have racism to deal with. It can destroy America. It can ruin all of us.

"You young people"—he looked first at David and then at Jeanette—"you young people are going to have it rough. There are no easy answers to the problems."

His lawyer had assured him that his case would never come to trial. His reputation as a good employee, a home owner, and a responsible citizen would protect him. But he would still have a record in the police files.

The Lenoirs did not stay long. They promised to keep in touch with the Williamses by telephone.

At six o'clock the governor declared a state of emergency. At the same time National Guard trucks rolled into the east side; squads of soldiers were posted at every corner for an area ten blocks square. Sentries in battle dress, with steel helmets and field boots, walked their posts, bayonets fixed. Some of the guardsmen who were colored patrolled near their own homes. Between the soldiers and the people there was no unofficial conversation.

The governor went on the air and pledged the full weight of his office to maintain and enforce the law. A curfew would be imposed from eight o'clock until sunrise. All meetings, including religious services, were prohibited during that time. The governor gave specific and general warnings.

Monday morning radio news reported that the national guard was in complete control. During the night all movement had been checked. No crowds had assembled. Guardsmen had been fired upon by snipers, and they had returned the fire. Two persons had been killed: one was a woman, the other a four-year-old girl. Outside the curfew area some fires had been started by Molotov cocktails.

The mayor and the governor called upon all citizens to resume their normal tasks, to go to their jobs and about their business. They promised that the authorities would be seeking to find the causes of the trouble, to remove them, and especially to prosecute those who had been apprehended in illegal activities.

David was anxious to resume his normal tasks.

He left the house earlier than usual, walking rapidly. He was confident that he was able to deal with the conflicts that had plagued him for so long. Mr. Lenoir had said, "No easy answers." Well, David would find them.

As he walked south on Main Street, he was thinking that he would know what to say when he talked things over with Sam and the clerks who were white at the hardware store. He would say that the people were angry and that they had lost their heads. He would point out that many of them were unemployed and that they were discouraged and frustrated, that they had been hurt and were seeking revenge.

At Twenty-sixth Street he considered his friend, John Bowman. He would tell John that now he could see the whole picture, he was even more determined to take his rightful place in America as a man. He would say that the goal of full citizenship for all would be achieved by colored and white people working together, side by side, rather than by fighting in the streets.

At Twenty-seventh Street he saw some unusual activity two blocks ahead. Firefighting equipment was in the street. He stopped, took a step back, then leaned forward and broke into a run.

Sam's hardware store was a blackened cavern, with white enameled pieces strewn around like scattered bones. In the paint section, where the cans had burst from the heat, the oils and spirits had burned. Through the black of soot, paint of various colors had streaked and spread in sunburst patterns.

Firemen with chemical extinguishers moved about the steaming and smoking shambles. A captain walked, book in hand, beside Sam. As he shook his head from side to side, Sam tried to answer the fireman's questions. His movements were jerky. It was as though he were a mechanical part of the scene. In his eyes he carried the look of a boxer out on his feet.

Without being told to do so, Big John Bowman went to work. With David helping and with the other clerks he set out to board up the yawning front, which had been enclosed by plate glass. Heavy-duty plywood and two-by-four framing had to be cut and fitted. John measured and marked the lumber, and when the other clerks had cut it with electric saws hooked up to a neighbor's outlet, he pounded in the nails with great force. David kept close to him, holding, carrying, removing broken sections, and doing the many things that needed to be done. He tried to keep his mind on the tasks as he performed them. He could not help but realize that his own job had gone up in smoke and that he, along with Sam Silverman and Big John and Jeanette and her parents, and the many others injured, killed, bereft of property and of loved ones, were all victims of the greed and terror and hatred and fear that had for so long been a blot on America.

Neither he nor John voiced an opinion.

With each panel nailed in as they worked across the front, less sunlight reached into the blackened interior. Sam walked out. For a while he only stood and watched.

In a moment, when the whining of the electric saws was silenced and John paused in his hammering, Sam said, "That's all right."

His voice was calm. David turned and looked at him. Sam's face showed no emotion, only concentrated interest as he said again, "That's all right."

Big John explained his plan to board up and seal the wide double door. Sam nodded his approval.

When Sam spoke again, David thought he was talking more to him than to anyone else.

"Everything looks bad just now," he said, "but don't let it get you down. Sometimes just living through your trouble is success, just not giving up, just not quitting."

David knew what Sam meant.

Afterword

When I was young, I didn't know my father was a great writer. During my early years, he worked as a teacher and a social worker; and I recall how he would often come home after a long day's work and sit at his desk far into the night, working on his books and stories. It was not until years later that I began to realize the magic he created on his typewriter.

Lorenz Graham was a pioneer in children's literature. He was the first African American writer to portray African Americans realistically in his books. Books had been written about well-known African American heroes and heroines, and other books had been written portraying blacks as deprived and hopeless. But my father took a completely different approach in his books.

He felt America should know about the lives and experiences of ordinary African Americans. So he wrote about a young man and his family—a family who struggled hard to overcome the injustices and hardships of the troubled times in which they lived. The Williams family was courageous and strong. In spite of all the problems they encountered, they never lost hope that the future would be better.

My father's readers enjoyed these novels about David Williams and his family. After each of the books reached the public, he received letters from people asking him to write another book because they wanted to know what happened to David next. Thus, the "Town" novels developed, spanning several decades in the life and experiences of David Williams.

The books in this series brought numerous honors and awards to my father. His greatest satisfaction, however, came from spreading his message that when people of different backgrounds understand one another, there is greater opportunity to achieve peace and harmony in the world.

Ruth Graham Siegrist, Ph.D.